I Haven't Been Myself

a novel

Nicole Palermo

Published by Midnight Ocean Press

ISBN: 979-8-9946708-0-4

Cover design by Clint English

clintenglish.com

Edited by Gary Jukes

Printed in the United States of America and other countries

For R, M and R

Always be yourselves

One

The night air is cold, but not frigid.

My teeth clench, pressing together futilely as if they're trying to retain some of my body's warmth.

It's only a 30-minute walk, but I left my sweater behind at the party. I hadn't planned to leave so abruptly.

Sighing heavily, I watch my breath crystallize in front of me. It spreads outward, then vanishes. In a way, it's beautiful. It sparkles in the icy darkness.

She pushed me past my breaking point, though my tolerance is low. I don't like being called out, forced out of my comfort zone. Wendy is usually sensitive to this, but when she's been drinking, she gets confrontational.

I know she means well, but I'm not exactly what others call 'open-minded.'

Walking home is probably for the best; she shouldn't be driving anyway.

I cross my arms, wishing I had my sweater. At least I had the good sense not to wear heels tonight. My footsteps are nearly silent on the dark country road.

Looking up, I'm grateful there's a moon, and I'm not relying on my cell phone flashlight to see.

I'm not afraid of the dark, but I'm scared of what lurks inside it. Not werewolves or vampires, but people. There are very few I trust.

Wendy is one of the rare people who have breached the high walls of protection I've built around myself.

Tonight is an exception, and I feel more alone than ever.

The bare trees lining the road rustle in the slight breeze. I hug myself a little tighter, trying to stay warm.

Damn it, why did I let Wendy drag me to Megan's house? It's much further outside of town than I want to walk in late fall, especially in the dark.

I could be home right now in my sweats, curled up on the couch with my dog, Maisie, and a glass of wine.

I see the headlights long before I hear the car pulling up behind me. The beams distort my shadow, stretching it in front of me like a ghost from my past.

I whip around, my long hair flying across my face. After shoving it back behind my ear, I clench my fists.

I'm still angry, ready to tell Wendy she has no business driving and to go home.

I freeze, realizing I don't know the approaching vehicle, and with the bright lights, I can't see the driver.

I begin to sweat, despite the cold.

I don't like surprises.

The car rolls up beside me, a black sedan. I don't immediately recognize the woman driving.

"Hey, need a ride?" she says.

I look at her curiously, and she leans across the seat. She's opening the passenger door. As she bends forward, the moonlight spills over her face.

I think I've seen her before, but I can't place her.

As if sensing my hesitation, she says, "I'm Mina. I don't think we've ever actually met, but I'm a friend of Megan's. You shouldn't walk all the way back to town in November. You don't even have a jacket."

Looking ahead at the long, dark road home, I shiver. Am I really considering accepting a ride from a stranger?

Glancing back at her, I realize how cold and exposed I am.

Is this really a good idea?

It goes against every instinct I have, but I silence the alarm going off in my head.

Climbing into the passenger seat, I'm thankful that the heat is blasting.

She came from Megan's party, too. It should be safe enough.

Shivering, I start to extend my hand, but a handshake would be awkward. I quickly tuck my arms back around myself.

Instead, I say, "I'm Leah. Thanks for stopping."

I take a closer look at Mina. Her features are sharp but attractive, and her short blonde hair is the direct opposite of my own long, dark hair.

I used to be blonde, a long time ago. I know it's a silly thing to miss, but sometimes you need to leave your past behind.

I have definitely seen Mina around, but don't recall seeing her tonight. There were a lot of people at Megan's house, so it's not strange that we didn't run into each other.

"You left early, too?"

She seems stiff, like she's uncomfortable that I accepted the ride. "I don't drink much, and it was getting too rowdy for me. Lucky for you, I guess. You would have been half frozen by the time you got back to town."

She taps the gas pedal and we start to move.

There's an awkward moment as neither of us knows what else to say.

I clasp my hands and look at the floor.

She stares straight ahead.

Mina finds words first. "So, how do you know Megan?"

I don't really want to make small talk, but I know I owe this woman that much. She did save me from walking home in the cold darkness of an approaching New England winter. "I don't, at least, not well. She's a friend of my friend, Wendy. I was dragged out tonight, and it's now obvious I should have stayed home. How about you?"

Her eyes are on the dark road ahead, but she briefly looks my way and replies, "Oh, I've known Megan forever. We went to the same school when we were kids and even worked together at FoodMart for a while in high school." She pauses.

A moment passes, and she continues, "I'm in town for a bit, visiting family. Megan invited me to stop by. Tonight made it clear why I moved away. Some people never change." She goes quiet again, running her fingers through her cropped hair.

And some people have a complete and total transformation.

I turn back to the passenger window, taking in the darkness rushing past us.

Best to keep those thoughts to myself.

I look over and catch Mina glancing from the road back to me.

Shifting uncomfortably, I fiddle with my ring, the small silver band my grandmother gave me at graduation.

The car smells strongly of vanilla. It's not unpleasant, but since I'm on high alert, it turns my stomach.

"Where am I dropping you off?" she asks, tapping the steering wheel while giving me a quick look.

I blink, realizing that the ride is nearly over. Maybe she wasn't watching me; she was waiting for me to tell her where to stop.

This was so much quicker than the walk would have been.

"You can drop me at the end of Tavern Street." I live on Rowan, but I don't voluntarily tell anyone that. I'll walk the extra quarter-mile to preserve my intentional solitude.

Mina pulls up to Tavern Street and takes the right-hand turn, insisting that she can drop me at my door. It's "no big deal."

I point to a building, showing her where to stop.

For a fraction of a second, confusion flickers across her face. Then it's gone, replaced by a smile as she wishes me goodnight.

I get out and thank her, then walk up the steps.

Everything in me hopes she'll drive away.

She doesn't, so I force a smile, wave and turn the knob.

It opens, and I step inside.

My heart is pounding, trying to escape my chest.

The door swings open into a small, shabby foyer with yellowed walls and worn linoleum flooring. To my left is a wall lined with tenants' mailboxes. Directly in front of me is an inner door with buzzers to ring each of the six apartments. The wall to the right has a bulletin board lined with "Missing Cat" posters and a note threatening the neighbor in apartment 2B for making noise after quiet hour.

The room itself is mercifully empty. A small window sits to the left of the outer door. I step over and look out, hoping that Mina has driven away.

She hasn't.

Her car is still at the curb, and she's on her phone. She's talking animatedly as she squints at the surrounding buildings.

I feel trapped. This tiny room is claustrophobic, and someone could enter at any moment. I take a breath and slowly count to three as I exhale. My heart rate slows, but my nervousness doesn't entirely dissipate.

Peeking back outside, Mina is still there.

I put my back to the wall and sink to the floor, contemplating my life choices.

This foyer isn't heated—the cold sinks in fast when you stop moving.

I think back to our brief conversation in the car. It's odd. She doesn't strike me as someone who grew up in a small town. She's unlike any of the people I've met since I moved here just over two years ago.

Mina's entire demeanor is almost... professional, and even without knowing Megan well, I can't picture them ever having been friends.

Megan is loud, vulgar and usually drunk. She works as a waitress at the only diner in town. As true as it is that people can change a lot in adulthood, they're quite an unlikely pair now.

My anger at Wendy subsided earlier as the burst of panic jolted through me, and I wish I could hear her voice. Taking out my phone, I send her a quick text.

Don't drive tonight. Call me tomorrow when you're home.

I know we'll work through tonight's argument. It's not the first time she's attempted to make me socialize, and it likely won't be the last. Thinking back to the party, I replay the scene in my head:

"Honestly, Leah, why are you so cold to people? He only wanted to get to know you. It would do you a lot of good to just relax and talk to someone other than me."

"You know I have no interest in meeting anyone. Not romantically, not socially. I'm fine right where I am."

"That's the thing, you AREN'T 'fine.' You're a walking billboard for therapy. What could it hurt to give another person a chance and get to know them? It doesn't have to be romantic, but you really need to lighten up and learn to live a little. Am I going to be your only friend for the rest of your life?"

With that, I'd turned on my heels and stormed out the door. My anger reared its head because, even after two years of friendship, she doesn't understand me. She knows me better than anyone else, and she still doesn't know me at all.

I'm past the anger now, but I'm disheartened. It isn't the first time we've argued like this, and she isn't wrong. It's complicated. Even if she is my best friend, there is so much she doesn't know about me because I won't, can't, fully open up to her.

I wearily check my phone and realize I've been sitting on the floor for nearly ten minutes. I stand and peek out the window, hoping with everything in me that Mina's gone.

She is.

I am finally safe to head home. I breathe a huge sigh of relief and let everything relax. I hadn't realized how tense I was.

Reaching for the doorknob, I start to turn it, and the door pushes open.

I fall back, startled.

A short, balding man, about 50 years old, enters and appears shocked to see a very panicked woman flailing in the foyer of his building at this time of night.

I regain my balance and rush past him, both embarrassed and terrified.

He stammers out a rushed apology.

The poor guy looked like he had seen a ghost, but my fight-or-flight response didn't let me do anything other than run.

Two

I don't stop running until I'm standing on my apartment porch, keys fumbling in the lock. My heart is racing from both the sprint and the encounter with the balding man, though I think I scared him as much as he scared me.

My place is in a four-unit building with its own entrance. I didn't want to live somewhere where I'd have to share space with my neighbors. I'm not much of a people person.

Maisie is barking on the other side of the door, and when I open it, she quiets and spins twice in a circle, tail wagging excitedly. She's ecstatic to see me in a way that only a canine companion can convey without words.

I lock the door behind me and sit on the floor just inside, letting Maisie curl up in my lap for pets.

I'm thankful for her companionship, but also for having her as my loyal protector. She's a small mixed breed I adopted from a local rescue when I moved here, but she is also my built-in alarm system. At 25 pounds, with her wiry hair and tongue constantly hanging out, she doesn't look very scary, but her presence comforts me in unexplainable ways.

As I sit stroking Maisie's back, I glance around my small apartment. It's become my safe space, the one place that I can let go and relax. There's a single bedroom, just big enough for my bed, dresser and a small end table with a decorative lamp. My kitchen has a few cabinets for dry goods and a sliver of countertop. The living room is a tiny nook that fits a small couch, a coffee table and my TV stand, which doubles as a bookshelf.

I don't watch much TV, but I do like to read. My bookshelf is full of non-fiction titles about people who have survived miraculous ordeals and come out the other side. I also have a library card to keep myself up to date on scientific trends. I love reading about where humanity is going and how we are shaping the next generation.

I take Maisie out to our small, fenced backyard, the only space that I share with my three neighbors. The fencing is low enough for me to see over it as I scan the wood line and the neighboring yards while she goes about her business.

There is still a light breeze that further chills the night air, so I'm glad to go back inside and lock up for the night.

I start my nightly routine, locking the doorknob and two deadbolts, just to be sure. I added the second one when I moved in. I double-check all six windows. They are closed and locked. We're on the second floor, and they haven't been opened in nearly two months, but I like to be certain.

I drink a small glass of warm water before bed. I'd like tea, but I'm too tired to wait for water to boil and still dehydrated from exertion and my moment of panic earlier.

Climbing into bed, Maisie curls up beside me and is asleep before I even pull up the covers. It's an ability I wish I had, too.

I lie in the darkness for a while, listening. Even though I live "in town," Ashbourne is still a rural area. Forests surround the entire outskirts, and every street is lined with trees. There is barely a house or apartment building that doesn't feel semi-private here.

Even with the windows locked up tight, I can hear an owl calling out in the dark. Whether it's seeking a mate or its next meal is unknown.

I roll onto my side in an attempt to get more comfortable.

Maisie snores lightly beside me, and I'm torn between deep affection for her and envy that she can fall asleep with no qualms whatsoever.

I'm a terrible sleeper. When I lie down, my mind races, processing the information I learned that day and turning it over and over in my thoughts. It's a real effort to quiet it enough to shut down for a few hours.

I have sleeping aids, but I hardly ever take them. I need the control of knowing that if the sounds in the night are something more than an owl, I'll have the presence of mind to act accordingly.

At last, I drift off into a fitful sleep. I don't usually dream, but I do tonight: of Wendy, of the balding man, of the rude neighbor in 2B.

I wake between each dream, and several other times as a branch cracks outside or a neighbor's dog barks. Finally, around 3 a.m., I fall into a deep sleep.

I'm dreaming again.

I'm six years old, and the smell of fresh bread permeates everything. Warmth from the last hours of daylight mixes with the oven's heat.

Drying herbs hang from the walls: a reminder of our day spent in her garden.

It's a scene of complete serenity, and I'm at home in every possible way.

Nan is stirring something fragrant on the stovetop, humming lightly. She turns and crosses the room. Taking my small hand and placing it on her heart, she says in her warm, throaty voice:

"Always remember, my girl: find your way home, and you will find your way forward."

This is a mantra she's repeated throughout my life. At six, I only knew that it felt good to bask in her comforting words.

The dream starts to change, and I am suddenly in the middle of the lake.

The water is cold, and I'm being pulled under with the weight of my clothes.

Wendy is standing on the shore, yelling something that I can't quite make out. It sounds like she's screaming "Let go!" but I'm not holding on to anything.

It dawns on me that I can shed my coat, so I remove it awkwardly in the water while trying to keep my head above the surface. I watch as it begins to float away.

Pushing it aside, I see Mina's face underneath the black water. Her short blonde hair floats like a halo around her. Her eyes are open, and the look on her face is accusatory. She reaches up and grabs me tightly by the ankle.

I kick and start to flail, looking for something, anything to grab on to. I try to scream and reach my hands upward toward the light of the moon as it echoes across the surface of the lake, but water fills my lungs as I'm carried down to the bottom.

I snap awake in a cold sweat, panting and shivering. The details of the dream were so vivid that I can still feel the cold water of the lake in my lungs.

I wonder if this dream was an anomaly or the start of a more ominous pattern. My subconscious seems to think that Mina is a threat, even though nothing noteworthy happened last night. Maybe silencing my inner alarms, even for a good reason, has psychological consequences I can't control.

My mind wanders back to the dream of my nan. My breath slows as I picture the joyous feeling of when I was just a child, dawdling in her kitchen after school or on the weekends.

The joy is bittersweet, as I haven't heard her voice or felt her comforting presence since I arrived in Ashbourne. It doesn't feel any more like home than it did years ago.

I replay what she said to me in the dream: *"Find your way home, and you will find your way forward."* It's nostalgic but hurtful, like pressing on a dark bruise. There is nothing I wouldn't give to start over. To be able to go home and sit in Nan's kitchen with the warmth of family and fresh baked goods spilling over my spirit, making me whole again.

I no longer have a home. I'm stagnant in this life, caught in a vicious circle of routine.

I think of being called *"Ellie"* by Nan. A lot of my family used that nickname, but Nan was the only one it ever felt right coming from.

Reaching over, I grab my phone off the nightstand— 5:30 a.m.

Even though it's an hour until daybreak, I know I won't be able to sleep another moment tonight. I drag myself out of bed, making sure Maisie, who is still snoring, isn't disturbed.

I change into workout gear and check my notifications. I have a text from Wendy:

"Stayng the inght @ Megs. Tlak tmrw" — sent around 2 a.m.

I'm glad she didn't drive and is safely asleep at Megan's house. I'm sure to hear from her later when she wakes up hungover; she'll probably want to get lunch.

I turn on the TV, lower the volume, and start an online yoga video. I do yoga or Pilates several times a week. It calms my mind and keeps me strong, but they're also the only types of exercise I can do in my tiny apartment without waking my neighbors.

I used to love running, but I can't have a treadmill on the second floor, and there is no chance I'm going to run outside when it's dark. The lack of people means a greater chance of running into the wrong ones. The few people who are out at 3 a.m. usually aren't the ones you want to run into.

I push myself hard, trying to rid my mind of my actions last night.

After the exhausting workout, I make a pot of coffee and a quick breakfast of eggs over easy with toast. I grab one of my newest library finds on gene editing and its implications for medicine over the next decade. It's a fascinating read, and time seems to melt away.

I look up. Maisie is sitting in front of me, practically electric with energy. I smile at her and look out the window. It's a beautiful morning.

It's almost nice enough to warrant opening the windows, but I don't.

Instead, I take Maisie outside, and we play fetch in the yard. Wearing her out is easy. Finally, she's bored and ready for a drink and a nap.

Her tongue lolls out of the side of her mouth, and she kisses me sloppily while I pet her.

She's a good girl, and so friendly.

Back inside, she has a long drink and then falls dramatically onto her bed with her stomach to the sky, seeking pets.

I laugh. "I know, your life is so tough, right, girl?" She gets the belly rubs anyway. She deserves them.

With Maisie worn out, I make another cup of coffee before taking a quick shower.

While the hot water rinses away my imagined transgressions, the events of last night play on an endless loop in my head.

A chill runs through me despite the hot shower as I remember the shock of lake water against my skin.

I hope this was a one-off. I'd rather not dream.

What was I thinking, accepting a ride from someone I don't know? Mina seems nice, but for all I know, she's a serial killer or one of those women who lure other women into sex work.

I smile, laughing at myself. Nothing about Mina screams "I'm recruiting for a pimp," and she dresses way too upscale to be a sex worker.

Just as my chuckles subside, my phone rings.

Looks like Wendy made it home. "Good morning, sunshine," I say, smiling. I'm glad to hear from her. Knowing she's home and okay allows me to relax.

"Ugh," she complains in my ear. "I should have slowed down after our argument. Instead, I went harder, and I'm regretting it today. Want to meet me for lunch at the diner?"

We agree to meet at noon, so I still have about 90 minutes to get myself dressed and ready for the day.

I make just one more cup of coffee and grab my tablet for a glance at the news before getting ready for lunch. I've trained myself to read, at a minimum, the headlines, both local and global. As cut off from the world as I am, I like to at least stay up to date on current events.

You never know what information you might miss if you aren't paying attention.

At any other time of the year, the diner is a casual 10-minute walk from my place. With the temperature just below freezing this morning, I drive instead.

My car is reliable, but old and rusty. The salted roads from the snowy winters aren't kind to cars. My income isn't high, but I make sure to maintain my vehicle's drivetrain; dependable transportation is essential.

I park, lock the car and walk up to the door. It's set up like a sixties diner, though that's probably because that's when it was built, rather than an aesthetic choice. Everything is chrome or striped, and the circular barstools at the counter spin all the way around. Overall, though, the place looks worn down and weary.

Wendy is already sitting at a booth toward the back. She's got coffee and a milkshake and looks slightly worse for wear. She's still half-wearing last night's makeup, and her mascara has migrated below her eyes. It makes her look even more tired than she likely is. Even in her hungover state, Wendy is a strikingly beautiful woman.

She has long, naturally curly auburn hair, currently thrown up into a large, messy bun on top of her head. Her translucent green eyes are the color of springtime moss, and they sparkle when she says something mischievous or when she thinks she's funny.

She's hands-down one of the smartest people I've ever met. She spent years training to become a pharmacist but suffered severe burnout from the stress. Taking the opportunity to move back home, she's been able to clear her head and reclaim her sanity.

A few years ago, she opened a local pharmacy and apothecary called "Roots and Remedies," where she fills prescriptions and also sells natural migraine remedies and skin salves. The homeopathic angle isn't a huge money maker, but the place pays her bills and has brought her more happiness than her high-pressure life ever did.

It isn't a stretch to see how someone who planned to be a doctor could have ended up selling homeopathic and organic wellness treatments to the people of her hometown.

Wendy loves people. She loves starting conversations with strangers and giving a well-placed compliment. In general, she likes to care for people. I think that after her collapse from the stress of city life, she realized that caring for others doesn't need to be flashy.

I slide into the bench across from her, and she smiles at me tiredly, tilting her head in an attempt to read my residual anger from last night. She knows me better than anyone else and can see, without exchanging words, that I'm not holding on to the argument.

Searching my eyes for lingering signs of annoyance, she quietly says, "I'm sorry about last night. Did you have to walk home?"

I shake my head slightly. "It's okay. You weren't entirely wrong. I just didn't want to hear it. I know I reacted badly. I started out walking, but luckily Mina picked me up and gave me a lift back to town. She left Megan's shortly after I did."

Wendy gives me a puzzled look. "Mina who?"

The world starts to compress around me, as if I'm being squeezed by an invisible force. "I'm not sure. She said she's known Megan since high school. That's actually the only reason I got in the car."

Wendy looks at me as surprise registers on her face. "I am actually shocked you got into a vehicle with someone you hadn't background checked. In triplicate."

I roll my eyes, even though she's right.

She gazes at the ceiling and purses her lips while thinking. "It was a big high school. I know it's a small town, but the high school kids attend a regional school, so our graduating class was close to 500 people. Still, you'd think I'd know her name through Megan."

With this new information, I breathe, and the world expands again, just slightly. I relay the info Mina gave me about being back in town for a short time, and Wendy shakes her head, signaling that she still isn't sure who Mina is.

"Maybe Mina is a nickname she picked up as an adult?"

Wendy's speculation is plausible. Many people have nicknames as kids and choose something different as adults to sound more mature or to change their image. Once you make your way into adulthood, your name symbolizes who you are.

Our waitress checks in, and I order a chef salad and a Dr. Pepper.

Wendy asks for a burger and fries to "soak up the alcohol."

I'm absolutely stealing a fry or two off her plate when it shows up. I know she won't mind.

Wendy asks if anything during the short drive seemed off or weird, since she knows I'm attuned to notice minor inconsistencies.

I tell her that Mina didn't give me any strange vibes, but I regale her with my tale of the apartment building on Tavern Street and the man I terrified with my neurotic tendencies.

Wendy throws her head back and laughs as I explain how I practically stampeded him in my attempt to race home.

I don't tell her about the dreams.

We eat our lunch while making small talk about the party, and I swipe about half a dozen fries. Consider it a toll for almost making me walk home in the dark.

The conversation turns to how her shop is doing, and when I ask, she lights up.

"I've found a vendor that sells that tea I adore for allergy season at a reasonable price, which was such a win. And I'm very close to making a deal with a local who makes an herbal tincture for insomnia." She takes a quick sip of her drink. "Those will both help so many people."

"I'm also considering having an 'open house' sale after Thanksgiving. I'm thinking I'll stay open late one night, offer 10 percent off and have hot apple cider and snacks available. Just to get people in the door and socialize a little to kick off the holidays."

She gets so excited to talk about her shop, and I wish I had something in my life that excited me that way.

"Oh! I almost forgot," she says, reaching into her bag and pulling out a small bottle. "I need you to test out this tea tree oil for me. I got a few samples, and I'm considering stocking it, but I want your highly critical opinion." She laughs, loving every minute of teasing me. "How is work going for you, by the way?"

She knows I hate my job. I work at Sanderson's General Store in the town center. I do everything from running the register to stocking shelves. I even occasionally help Bill Sanderson, the owner, figure out his taxes.

I've also had to sort out his books a few times to keep him out of trouble.

It pays next to nothing, but most of the year it's a five-minute walk, and I don't have to socialize too much. I'm sure that most people know me as "the grumpy cashier" at the store, but that's okay with me. I don't need more friends.

"Work is work," I tell Wendy. "It pays the bills, and Bill is nice, if a little unorthodox."

He's a really strange man. An aging widower who probably hasn't had a home-cooked meal in the 10 years since his wife passed, he's taken to "painting by numbers" as a hobby.

The store's walls are decorated with his creations. A dolphin jumping out of the ocean graces the bathroom. There's a meteor falling as the startled dinosaurs look up to the sky in the break room, and a half rainbow over a lighthouse behind the register.

None of them are done well.

He also does a terrible job shaving and always misses a patch of facial hair.

Overall, though, he's a nice guy and a good boss. He's probably the only other person in town that I have a friendly relationship with besides Wendy.

"I do have to work later today, till close," I say, finishing out my earlier thought. "I hope Brad isn't working."

I can't stand Brad. He's a close talker, and he asks too many questions. He's been at Sanderson's Store for a year and still hasn't gotten the hint that I don't want to be friends.

Wendy's mouth is full of burger, but she crosses her fingers to signal she's on my side.

Walking out to the car together after lunch, we agree that she'll come to dinner at my place the day after tomorrow.

I love to cook, and it's pretty easy to make tasty food for myself, even on a limited budget.

I also love to bake, but I reserve it for special occasions. Measuring the ingredients, leveling them off, and turning all the separate pieces into something special is soothing. There's nothing quite like taking something you created out of the oven and it being *perfect*.

Art, made from science.

Three

I decide to go out this afternoon to get groceries, since I'm working the next two days.

After quickly stopping at home to let Maisie out, I make the 10-minute drive to FoodMart. I get most of my groceries from Sanderson's, but they generally only have staple food items and nothing special.

Pulling into a space near the front of the store, I check the time on my phone. I have at least an hour for shopping, which is more than enough time to get my purchases home before work. I walk through the sliding doors, and a blast of heat hits my face. It's comforting in a way that feels familiar. I used to love grocery shopping, but I avoid the bigger, more crowded stores these days.

I start my shopping in the dry goods section, looking for the right rice to make risotto and a bone broth to cook it in. Next, I find the perfect cheese, then salmon. I finally round out the meal with some asparagus (and it's on sale!).

I push my cart to the baking aisle to get the ingredients for a gingered peach galette. It's one of my favorite desserts, and it always reminds me of Nan. It's a warm comfort food that brings me back to happier times.

I'm examining a jar of candied ginger when, in my peripheral vision, I pick up on movement at the end of the aisle. Leisurely carrying a basket and stopping to look at the pancake mix is Mina.

I freeze. She hasn't seen me yet—my mind races. I could duck out and avoid her until she heads to the cash registers.

I contemplate a second too long, and she looks up. I'm caught, and there is no avoiding conversation now. I'm strangely relieved that she saw me, and the choice was taken out of my hands.

It's a feeling I'm not used to. I typically like control over every situation.

Looking back at the candied ginger in my hand, I study it, decide it's the right one, and place it in my carriage. When I look up again, Mina has crossed half the distance between us, a small smile on her face. As she approaches, I realize she's much taller than I would have guessed when we were sitting in her car. She must be at least 5'9".

My mind races with what to say. For quite a while, all my socialization has been with Wendy. I'm not sure how to talk to anyone else. Our awkward conversation last night in the car is evidence enough of that.

As I'm preparing a clumsy conversation in my mind, I feel a warm hand on my arm.

I jump, shocked that I'm being touched. Someone snuck up on me; I'm losing my edge.

I turn quickly, removing the unknown hand from my body and see it's Carla Morrow. She's a customer who is always at Sanderson's. Sometimes she's shopping and other times just hanging around, as small-town people tend to do.

Carla is about 40 years old, though she looks haggard, like she's seen more than most who have lived her lifetime. She's much shorter than I am, only about five feet even. She's only a few inches taller than her daughter, Lilly, who is eight.

Carla is always wearing clothing with lots of pockets. Large pockets, some of which hold notebooks or pencils, a wallet or gum and candies. She doesn't carry a purse, so she wears her everyday items on her body.

"How are you, dear?" she asks kindly. "Doesn't Sanderson pay you enough to shop at his store? I know he's more expensive than FoodMart, but don't you get a discount?" She laughs at her own joke.

I smile tightly, ready to be done with this conversation. I look over and see Mina is now browsing the flour section directly next to me, trying not to eavesdrop. I have the distinct feeling that she doesn't actually need flour.

I look back at Carla. "I'm well, Carla. How are you and Lilly doing?"

Carla's face changes at the mention of her little girl, but she recovers quickly, and a cheerful smile crosses her face. "She's doing well! She's in the candy aisle getting herself a treat and should be along any minute."

Lilly rounds the corner a moment later, clutching a bag of gummy bears.

Her long blonde hair sways as she limps toward us, and by the time she reaches us, she's wheezing. She's had the limp as long as I've lived here, but I don't ask about it. It seems personal.

"Oh, Lilly, honey!" Carla exclaims, searching in her many pockets for Lilly's inhaler. She locates it, but in the process, manages to dump out a full pocket of belongings. The inhaler hits the floor, along with a datebook, a pair of safety scissors and a small paperback novel.

She deftly picks every item up from the floor, and hands the inhaler to Lilly, who promptly takes a long breath in and then another. Her wheezing subsides, and she smiles.

Lilly is a good kid, but she makes me uncomfortable. All children do.

"Hi, Lilly," I say. Turning back to her mother, I add, "Nice to see you, Carla. I won't keep you from your shopping. Have a nice day."

Carla tells me not to be silly and starts chattering about how well Lilly is doing at school, how she can't believe steak is so expensive now and how she heard that Sanderson's is going to stock calendars for the holiday season.

She homeschools Lilly, so I smile despite myself. Of course she thinks Lilly is doing great; she's the teacher.

Lilly looks uncomfortable, aware of my discomfort as Carla continues talking at me, to nobody in particular.

Suddenly, Mina is standing there, towering over Carla. "Hi, Leah," she says cheerfully. "Can I get your help with something? I need a bag of flour, and I don't know the difference between the brands." She glances at Carla and asks, "Sorry, am I interrupting?"

Carla looks up at Mina and realizes that our conversation is over. She takes Lilly's hand and gives me a hasty goodbye, not even answering Mina's question. She and Lilly walk away at the fastest pace that her daughter's limp will allow.

After watching them turn out of the aisle, I move back toward Mina and say, "What are you baking? The flour only makes a real difference for specific dishes."

She chuckles and says, "I don't actually need flour. I have no idea how to bake. You just looked like you'd rather be anywhere else, and she was holding you hostage in conversation."

I let out a short laugh myself. "Thank you, Mina." My shoulders relax unconsciously. "Carla is nice but has no filter and does not know when or how to make a graceful exit."

Mina nods, then glances at my cart and sees the ginger and peaches. "Looks like you know how to use flour, though. Making dessert?"

I feel my cheeks flush slightly. Not at the question itself, but because she's disarmed me and I'm unsure exactly how. Her peek into my cart feels personal. I don't relax around anyone except Wendy. I just met Mina yesterday. Why do I have such a strong feeling that I can trust her? Maybe I really am losing it.

"I'm making dinner this week for Wendy," I tell her.

She nods again, then, with a smirk, asks me if I need a ride home.

I smile, disarmed. "No," I say. "I drove myself. No more rides with strangers."

"That's good to hear. It's important to protect yourself."

She isn't wrong. I want to press her for more information about how she knows Megan, but I can't think of a way to do it without making her repeat her story. Will another inquiry be both awkward and redundant?

I look at what's in her basket. She's got two TV dinners and a six-pack of beer. Something here feels off, and the distrustful part of me rears its head.

"TV dinners, huh? The family you're staying with doesn't cook?"

For the first time, Mina looks surprised, like I caught her in something I wasn't supposed to know. This time it's she who blushes. "My relatives are out to dinner tonight, and I can't even boil water without the smoke alarm going off."

I hesitate slightly too long trying to make sense of her explanation, and she ends the conversation, seemingly relieved. "Okay, well, see you around, Leah."

Damn, I lost my chance for inquiry. "Thanks again for chasing Carla off. See you later."

Mina leaves the aisle, and I'm left standing there, wondering how I became so awkward with other people.

My conversation with Mina made me forget to grab an extra bottle of wine. I had passed her once more near the checkout, and we shared one of those awkward smiles that happen when you've already said goodbye to someone but run into them again before leaving.

Two hours later, I'm sitting behind the register at Sanderson's, practically dying of boredom. I have my elbow on the counter with my chin propped up on one hand.

Bill is in the back, working on a new canvas of the night sky and bats. He's not getting any better at it, despite all the time he puts in.

He lives upstairs but spends most of his waking hours in the shop, "supervising." This means he occasionally pokes his head out of the back to check in, more often when I'm working alone.

I appreciate this because even though Bill isn't my "friend," I've become accustomed to him, and I trust him in the limited way I trust anyone.

He doesn't understand me, but he knows how much I hate people, so if it sounds like someone is giving me a hard time, he will step in and handle it with exuberant cheeriness that he knows I don't have.

It's a slow night, and the shop is dead. We're usually busier on weekdays when people are stopping in for a gallon of milk or a can of peas. Really, any time they don't want to go all the way to FoodMart for something that they can quickly pick up on their way home.

Saturdays are busy because we also have gifts and mementos. Locals will stop in to see what's new and pick up items for birthdays or upcoming holidays. We also sell some locally made soaps, jams and handmade items that tourists buy as souvenirs.

Bill has a section of his paintings for sale, but nobody ever buys them.

We're open until 9 p.m., so I have three more hours of devastating boredom to look forward to before I can go home.

Bill pops his head out to check on me. "Everything going okay out here?"

"Yup, everything's great, Bill. We're all clean and stocked, and I'm just killing time. How is the newest painting going?"

"Pretty good, pretty good. I think I'm starting to get the hang of how to make a shadow look different than contrast."

"Good to hear," I say. He most definitely is not getting the hang of it.

The minutes tick slowly by, and a man comes in to buy a cheap bottle of wine. A woman runs in and out looking for brown rice. Two teenagers linger by the beer case, but ultimately each buys a candy bar before moving on. I turn around and stare at the painting of the lighthouse that looks more like a melting cigarette, trying to pinpoint the exact moment my life took this detour into obscurity.

The door opens, and Carla walks in with Lilly. I internally groan about as hard as someone can, silently.

Carla comes over to me while Lilly goes to check out the scented candles that came in yesterday for the holidays.

"Hi, Carla. How are you? Something you need help with?" I ask about as flatly as possible, signaling how much I *don't* want to chat.

Carla cozies up to a stool at the counter, ready to make the rest of this shift, somehow, more unbearable. "I'm doing well, dear, thanks for asking. I don't need anything, just trying to get Lilly out of the house, you know, fresh air and all. Kids these days spend far too much time in front of screens. Not my Lilly! Even with her ailments, we don't just sit around." Carla smiles her too-big smile at me, and my annoyance shifts to discomfort.

"Yeah," I counter, not really knowing what else to say.

"Lilly is quite a trooper," Carla continues. "You know, there was a point where the doctors weren't sure if she would even make it, but here she is! Isn't it funny how much of life is just chance?"

Of all the odd people I know, Carla just may be the strangest. I wonder if she's always been like this, or if motherhood changed her.

"Sure," I say, getting down off my chair and starting to sift through things under the counter, trying to avoid making eye contact and additional painful conversation.

It doesn't stop her. "So, any big plans for the holidays? Where are you from, anyway? I know you've been here a few years, but I only ever see you with that woman who runs the pharmacy. Don't you have family? You're young to be completely on your own."

I stiffen, and as I begin my frequently rehearsed answer, the door swings open. Carla and I both look up.

A woman in her early twenties steps inside, followed a few seconds later by an older man with a scalp so clean-shaven that it reflects the fluorescent lights. They don't appear to be together. She heads for the section with allergy medicine and Band-Aids, and he stops near the canned soups.

With nothing remarkable happening, Carla turns back to me to continue her line of questioning.

Before she can get out another word, the young woman finishes browsing and approaches the counter. "Hi," she says. "Do you have any rash cream in the back? There's nothing on the shelves."

I shake my head. "No, everything we have is out front. Our stock shipments come in on Thursday."

She looks worried and slightly annoyed. "Ugh, I don't know what I'm going to do. I had this reaction to a new lotion, and now my entire upper body is covered in this." She lifts her sleeve, and I can see a very large red rash covering her arm. "It's so itchy, and Root closed early tonight." It looks like it will be miserable to attempt to live with until Root reopens tomorrow.

I think for a moment. "I may be able to help," I tell her.

Getting up, I motion for her to follow me. We walk through the aisles, sidestepping the other patrons. I hand her apple cider vinegar and baking soda, then break off a leaf from the aloe vera plant Bill keeps near the door. I also grab the mini bottle of tea tree oil Wendy gave me from my purse.

In a plastic cup from the break room, I start adding what seem like reasonable amounts of each ingredient. Grabbing a spoon, I start mixing, slowly at first to incorporate everything, then more quickly to turn it into a paste.

Once the texture seems right, I take a small amount and put it on my own arm to make sure it doesn't burn my skin.

After a minute, I'm satisfied that this thrown-together remedy, at worst, won't hurt her. I hand her the half-full cup and tell her to put some on a small patch to see if it helps.

She looks curious and takes the cup from me, dabbing a small amount on the underside of her wrist. After about fifteen seconds, her eyes widen. "It works! This actually works!"

She takes a larger dollop of the homemade cream and starts to slather it over both arms. She breathes out a huge sigh as relief hits her. "Oh my God, thank you! Thank you SO much!"

She leans in to hug me, and I stiffen, but attempt to half-wrap an arm around her. We share an awkward embrace. She pulls back, a genuine smile on her face. "I don't know what I would have done if I had to live like this until tomorrow. You have no idea how much I appreciate this!" She pays for the ingredients and takes her cup of improvised rash cream home.

I've drawn a lot of attention by helping the woman, and have generated a small crowd of people hovering, watching me, waiting to see the outcome. I'm not even sure where they all came from. Did this many people even come in?

Now they're all looking at me, some in wonder, others in bewilderment. An old woman I haven't seen before nods approvingly and says, "It's nice to see young people still using the old remedies." The group murmurs in agreement as many of them disperse to find what they came in for.

Bill pokes his head out of the back room and sees that a small line of people has formed at the register. He looks at me and asks, "Do you need help?"

"No," I answer, "I'm good. I'll cash these guys out."

He seems relieved not to have to step away from his hobby and disappears out back.

I work through the short line. Most people don't make large purchases, which is normal here. The line is gone in under five minutes, and I'm left alone with my thoughts.

Wait, no.

Carla is still here. Terrific. She and Lilly had been sitting in the little waiting area where locals tend to hang out when they have nothing going on. Now that the store is empty again, she moves back toward her seat at the counter.

"That was some show you put on," she says. "Where did you learn to do that?"

I'm slightly embarrassed to have made a spectacle of myself. I wasn't trying to, I just felt bad for the woman with the rash. "Oh, here and there," I say. "My grandmother made lots of natural remedies." I don't let on that she isn't the only person who taught me what I know.

Carla gives me a hard look and adds, "I hope you know what you're doing. You could really hurt someone if you make a mistake."

I'm shocked because her comment sounded deeper than concern. Why is she upset about what happened tonight? Did I somehow offend her?

She registers that what she said was harsh, and she softens considerably. "I'm sure you do, dear. I'm sure you do. I didn't mean to imply otherwise." She backs away, then calls to Lilly. "Lilly, time to go home!" They exit, and Lilly lags a few paces behind Carla.

Before the door shuts behind them, Lilly turns to look at me over her shoulder.

She seems sad.

Four

I say goodbye to Bill, and he locks up behind me.

I wonder if he goes upstairs and continues painting, or if he has "home" hobbies that keep his mind busy.

I don't usually walk to work when I have a late shift, but after the confusing interaction with Mina at the grocery store, I needed to clear my head.

Walking in the cold, with the wind in your face, can be very cathartic. It feels less so now that I'm going home in the dark.

The town center has streetlamps, but once you get past Forest Street, you're on your own.

There is still a moon, and it looks as if someone poked a billion tiny pinholes in the otherwise black sky. I try not to think about the fact that I'm walking home in the dark. Again.

Why have I been making so many poor choices lately, and such dangerous ones? Is Wendy's influence slowly rubbing off on me? Tonight, I helped a stranger just because I could. What is happening to me?

I hear a scuffle in the woods. It's likely just a nocturnal animal hunting, but I feel tense. I'm still a couple of minutes from home. I consider running but settle on walking faster instead.

The night feels oppressive, like a jacket a size too small.

Suddenly, I hear what sounds like someone coughing. I freeze in my tracks, listening. It feels like someone is watching me, but I can't see or hear another soul. Ice runs up my spine as I wait, still and silent.

I peer down the dark, tree-lined streets, looking for a person or silhouette. I hope to see someone smoking a cigarette or standing on their porch, but there's nothing. Suddenly, I hear a sneeze, not ten feet to my right.

I don't wait around to find out who it was and start running. So much for my rule about not running in the dark; it seems to be becoming a habit.

In the safety of home, with Maisie curled up in my lap, I let myself relax. I know I overreacted. There was no reason to sprint away from someone who probably just has a cold. Just because I couldn't see them didn't mean they were hiding or watching me.

I stroke Maisie behind the ears and let the slow rhythm of her breathing guide my own.

It's difficult to be a person wound so tightly that everything in life feels like an attack. Always waiting for the worst to happen is exhausting.

I change into my comfiest sweats, wash my face and apply lotion.

Looking in the mirror, I see the stress of the last few years on my face. Fine lines are starting to appear on my forehead that weren't there before. Smile lines are missing altogether. You have to actually smile to earn them.

I pour a glass of wine and flip on the TV. I'm debating between *Seinfeld* and *The Office* for late-night reruns when Maisie starts to whine. She needs to go out. I sigh. I know that I need to take her, but I'm so comfortable and relaxed that I really don't want to. I have practically melted into the couch at this point.

I haul myself up and put my slippers on. It's cold, so I grab my jacket. The weight of it triggers the memory of my dream. Of Mina, cold and judging. Of being grabbed, dragged down to the bottom of the lake.

I shiver, trying to shake off the memory. I take Maisie outside and wait, but the unease has settled in.

There is less of a breeze tonight, which is a welcome reprieve. It also makes everything feel quieter. I hear a door slam in a neighboring apartment, which makes me jolt. I take a breath and tell myself that their anger is not directed at me.

Maisie is taking her sweet time, and I scan the perimeter of our yard looking for signs of trouble. Seeing nothing, I try to relax by rolling my shoulders a few times.

"Come on, Maisie, let's wrap it up," I encourage her. She finds a spot she's happy with, and we're both relieved. Suddenly, she goes very still. She's looking beyond the fence, ears perked up.

My breath catches in my chest. I hear a rustling sound in the woods that could be a deer or another large animal, or perhaps something more.

Maisie lets out a loud bark followed by a low growl. The rustling starts to move away from us, deeper into the woods. I grab her and dash back inside, triple-checking all the locks and the windows. Finally, I settle back on the couch, my heart still pounding.

I take a sip of wine and try to calm myself by wrapping my blanket tightly around me. After watching two episodes of *Seinfeld* and giving my nervous system a break, I decide to take something to help me sleep tonight.

I haven't heard another sound since our scare in the yard, and I'm *almost* fully convinced it was just an animal in the night, not a threat.

I go to the bathroom cabinet and reach for the bottle of sleeping pills. A therapist I saw a while back prescribed them. It's still nearly full, despite having had it for almost three years.

I hesitate. Being chemically out of control is scary in its own way. I unscrew the cap and take out a tablet, turning it over in my hand.

I swallow it quickly with a glass of water.

Decision made.

I let the burden of allowing my guard down to haunt me for just a moment, then I shrug and move to the bedroom.

Between the glass of wine and the sleeping pill, I fall asleep in under ten minutes. I sleep peacefully, without fitful dreams.

I wake the next morning, not remembering if I dreamed at all.

Five

Today, I feel more rested than I have in forever. I find myself humming while I shower. There's a strange lightness that has settled in me. I feel calm; it's unfamiliar.

The cool air outside feels good, and my muscles are still warm from my Pilates video.

The feeling is strange and almost alien.

I feel content, I realize with surprise. I live so much of my life on edge that this feeling is alien to me. But after a night's sleep and my planned dinner with Wendy tonight, I have something to look forward to. I'm happy.

I walk into Sanderson's with a slight smile on my face. I've surprised myself with this unusually good mood, and I hope I can make it through the day intact. I walk quickly to the break room to put away my coat and purse.

Staying in a good mood will be impossible; Brad is also working this morning.

Brad gives me the creeps. He's in his mid-20s, tall, and average-looking. Neither attractive nor ugly, but completely forgettable. When he introduces himself, you forget his name by the time you manage to peel yourself away from the conversation. He's nice enough, but he asks a lot of questions and doesn't quite understand personal space. I constantly find myself having to invent tasks when he's around. Otherwise, he'll hang out a foot too close while I try to escape. He's socially awkward and completely unaware of it.

Brad turns around when he hears my footsteps behind him and smiles. "Good morning, Leah! How are you? How was your weekend?"

I give him a tight smile and reply, "Good morning, Brad. It was good, thanks." I don't ask about his weekend in an attempt to stave off additional conversation, but as usual, he doesn't take the hint.

"Great to hear!" he says enthusiastically. "I did a lot of studying this weekend. Really hoping to finish classes by the middle of next year."

He's studying to be a therapist, which is ironic because he can't read people at all, and every emotion he shows feels practiced.

"That's great, Brad," I say, hoping he's done chatting. He isn't.

"I'm just finishing up a class focused on people who survive traumatic experiences but still suffer from PTSD."

I inhale sharply. Has he actually learned something in this class?

He's still looking at me. Why is he looking at me like that?

Brad tilts his head as if analyzing me, then adds his expert opinion. "You wouldn't understand, though. It's high-level clinical therapy stuff. Since you're just a retail worker, it would go RIGHT over your head."

I let my body relax and give him the first genuine smile I've ever given him. "You're right, Brad. I'm sure it's way beyond my comprehension." I laugh and don't bother telling him that I have a master's degree and nearly finished my PhD.

As boring as the day is, there's excitement in the air as Bill puts up the winter holiday decorations for the store. I offer to help him, but decorating is one of his favorite pastimes. I think it's why he paints, so that he can hang them up afterward.

It's one of the few times of year you'll see Bill up front instead of hiding out back.

The locals of Ashbourne love Bill. He's lived here most of his life, and Sanderson's has been open for over

30 years. I don't know why he spends so much time hiding. When he's visible to customers, they are excited.

It takes him three times as long to put up decorations as it should, because people interrupt him constantly to ask how he's doing, what he's up to for the holidays or to ask for advice on a product.

Bill is just a wholesome small-town guy, genuine to his core. I think it's why everyone loves him.

I pull myself out of my thoughts and smile. An older woman is laughing about something he said while her grandchild hangs off his leg.

He looks perplexed, like he isn't sure why what he said was funny. His face changes to delight, and he chuckles along with her.

She says goodbye, and Bill hangs one strand of pine garland before an older man comes up, slaps him on the back, then shakes his hand.

Bill smiles, and the whole process starts over again.

I watch as Bill navigates customers while decorating. I wonder again why he stays out back like a hermit when the community clearly enjoys his presence.

At lunch, Wendy and I share a bench outside. It's warm enough to be comfortable.

She meets my eyes, studying me.

"What?"

"You just seem more relaxed lately. What's been going on?"

I don't have a real answer to her question, so I feign ignorance. "What do you mean?"

Wendy looks at me like she's trying to decipher a foreign language that's written on my forehead. "So, you don't agree you've been more relaxed?" There's a tone of comedic affection in her voice.

I smile at her. "I agree; I guess I just haven't really thought about it. For starters, I haven't been quite as unlucky lately. That's a welcome change."

I'm historically, almost hilariously, unlucky. Ever since moving here, I have had minor inconveniences several times a week. It's usually small, like a customer spilling something on me right at the beginning of a shift. Sometimes it's my laundry disappearing out of the dryer, then turning back up the next day, soaked and smelly. My keys disappear and reappear just as I start to panic.

Lately, my stove has been lighting up as though a burner is on, even though I haven't used it. That one is creepy for obvious reasons, but I had facilities check it, and they say nothing is wrong.

None of this has happened for a few weeks now, and it's a welcome reprieve.

"I guess things have just been looking up. Maybe that's why I accepted the ride from Mina. It's easier not to be on edge when things aren't constantly happening to throw you off balance."

"True," Wendy says. "I'm glad." She grabs my hand and I flinch. "Sorry," she says. "Too much, too soon." She's teasing me.

I laugh and squeeze her hand. "It's a beautiful day, isn't it?"

She stares as if I have five heads. "It IS a nice day. But who ARE you, and what have you done with Leah?"

I laugh again. "I'm here. It's me. I actually slept last night. Maybe this is who I am when I'm not waiting for the other shoe to drop."

Wendy looks at me seriously. "Are you ever going to tell me more about your past? What the shoes look like, maybe?"

I tense. "Wendy, I…" I trail off.

"Sorry," she says, squeezing my hand. She gives me a quick smile before letting go and taking a bite of her wrap. "I know eventually you'll open up. I'll be here when you're ready."

"I'm really grateful to have you, Wendy. Thanks for understanding." I give her a small smile.

"No problem," she says through her mouthful of food.

After lunch, I'm cleaning some shelves at the back of the store, standing on a stepladder that's seen better days.

There's a lull as we hit mid-afternoon, when most people are working.

I stand on my tiptoes to reach the bottles at the very back. As I'm dusting the very last one, I hear someone clear their throat behind me.

Startled, I nearly lose my footing. I grab the shelf to steady myself.

Looking behind me, it's Carla and Lilly. I press my hands to my face and try to quiet my thumping heart with some deep breaths. After a few, I climb down from the ladder.

Brushing my hands on my pants, I ask, "Something I can help you with, Carla?"

She smiles at me. "I wanted to ask when your fancy Christmas chocolates will be in. I would think fairly soon?"

I sigh and put my hand on my heart, which is still beating overly fast. "Yes, I believe they'll be in next week's shipment, Thursday."

Carla's smile falters briefly. "You should be careful on that ladder. The shelf could have fallen on you." She goes back to grinning.

"No, it's really sturdy," I explain. I'm not sure why I'm defending a shelf. "Bill anchored it to the wall about eighteen months ago after a vendor bumped it accidentally and it nearly toppled over. It's not going anywhere."

Carla's smile fades for a moment, then returns full force. "Oh, that's great, dear. Glad to know Bill is keeping his staff safe!" Her smile widens, though it doesn't seem possible.

She is such an unusual woman, but she's nice enough. She makes me uncomfortable, but to be fair, so does anyone who tries to interact with me.

The rest of the workday passes without incident. Another day without a single unlucky moment.

Maybe the tide is turning?

Six

After work, I walk out to my car and realize one of
my tires is low.

"Ugh. Just what I need." Not the worst thing that can
happen, but so much for my lucky streak.

I sigh. Getting in, I drive to the closest gas station,
only about five minutes from Sanderson's.

Fumbling in my center console, I find two quarters:
just enough to start the tire pump.

That's lucky enough, I guess.

My rear driver's-side tire is visibly sagging, but the
others look fine. I'll have to keep an eye on that. If it
seems low again, I'll give the repair shop a call.

On the way home, I stop and pick up a pizza. I don't
eat a lot of takeout, but it feels celebratory. It's another
good day in the books, and that is something to honor.

As usual, Maisie is happy to see me, but I think she's
even happier to see the pizza.

We spend the evening relaxing, and it's a great end to
a pretty great day.

When I take Maisie out before bed, my heart beats
fast for a moment, but just because of the darkness and
the unknown noises it holds. By the time we're back
inside, it's settled again.

When it's time for bed, I wash my face, put on lotion
and change into pajamas.

Maisie is already curled up in her spot, asleep.

I'm so grateful for her. For Wendy, too.

I'm shocked as I realize I have Bill to add to that list.
He's grown on me in a way that I didn't expect. While

Wendy did her best to leap over my walls, Bill has somehow tunneled under them unintentionally.

I fall asleep easily tonight. It's a welcome change from my usual pattern.

I wake the next morning to another nice day. It's not unusual for New England in autumn. You never know what you're going to get. It could be 60 degrees and sunny, or 25 degrees with ice and snow.

I take Maisie outside and enjoy the slight breeze in my hair. Scanning the yard, nothing seems out of order. It's calming.

I'm working again today, so I have breakfast and coffee while skimming the news, then take a quick shower.

As I step outside, I realize I want to walk to work again today.

Wendy is right. Who am I?

Even a month ago, this wasn't something I would have considered. Now, here I am, choosing it.

The walk is soothing, and I arrive on time and in a good mood.

The workday starts fine. The store is bustling, and I'm busy checking out customers, stocking new specialty items, and keeping it clean.

During my lunch, I'm in the break room eating a sandwich when Bill comes to get me. He wants my opinion on his newest painting. He doesn't ask Brad because I don't think he likes Brad much either.

The bats look more like black flying squirrels. The night sky has a strange orange tone that doesn't belong in the dark. He tells me he screwed up one of the numbers and didn't realize it until halfway through, so he had to improvise. I tell him I think it's an overall improvement. If he loves painting, he should keep doing it.

I still have 10 minutes left of my lunch break, so I sit with Bill while he opens his next project. The box shows five cats, each a different color. They're sitting atop a fence, watching two bluebirds on a clothesline above.

Bill looks at me, then looks away. "I know I'm not good at this, Leah," he says. "But I want you to know how much I appreciate the kindness you've shown me. I know my paintings stink, but you always have a kind word."

A startled laugh escapes me; I can't help it. "What are you talking about, Bill?"

He shifts in his seat and then meets my eyes. "I'm terrible at painting. You know it, and I know it. But it helps me pass the time, and I enjoy it. It distracts me from thinking about Martha, and I figure it's better than sitting in front of a TV all day."

This is the first time Bill has ever opened up to me like this. It tugs on my heartstrings in a way that feels deeply human. It's foreign and familiar at the same time. Against my instincts, I reach out and put my hand over his. "I'm sorry, Bill. I didn't know this was how you were coping with Martha's passing. I'm sorry if I ever made you feel like your paintings aren't good."

I glance around at his hobby room, the walls covered in his creations, each of them a little sad in its own way—a lot like Bill himself.

He looks mildly amused. "I didn't need you to apologize, Leah. They do stink, but you've always been so supportive anyway."

I let out another laugh and squeeze his hand, just slightly. "I know I'm not much of a talker, but I am actually a great listener. If you ever want to talk about Martha, I'm here."

I spend the next 5 minutes of my break, and the first 15 of Brad's, listening to Bill talk about how he met his wife, and how much he misses her. It feels good to connect with someone over their past, without having to divulge any of my own.

I come away from the conversation with a better understanding of Bill than I've had in the years I've known him.

After my extended break, I relieve a visibly angry Brad. He's so mad that he doesn't even talk to me, which is a win in my book. When he returns, he's calmed down and is chatty again.

I'll have to remember to make him angry more often; it's worth a shot if it'll keep him quiet.

The afternoon is busy, and time slips away. It's nearly time to go home now. I'm counting down the last 15 minutes on the clock when a regular customer comes in. I say hi, and she smiles and moves past me to find what she came in for. She carries a sack of potatoes and some onions to the register, and I start to check her out. I can see her staring, so I look up.

"Are you the one who mixed up that cream for Shelly?" she asks.

I'm caught off guard, and I don't like the attention. I start to stutter out an answer, but Brad overhears and quickly comes up to the counter, delighting in the gossip.

"Hey, Kayla. What happened with Shelly?" he asks the customer.

She lights up, enjoying Brad's attention.

"The other day, she came in here with a nasty rash. This woman mixed up a rash cream from items inside the store. Shelly said it works better than anything she could have bought over the counter."

Words still fail me, as now Brad and Kayla are staring at me.

"That was you, wasn't it?" she asks again.

"Yeah," I say, with an uncomfortable laugh. "It was me. Where did you hear about that?"

She brightens again and says, "At Root today, it's all anyone is talking about."

I groan. That's all I need, to be the talk of the town. I liked being invisible much better.

"Where did you learn to do that?" Kayla presses.

I plaster on a polite smile. "My nan was good with home remedies. I just wanted to help." My mind races as I wonder who "everyone" that is talking about me today is.

I'm really not looking to become small-town famous.

"It's super cool that you can heal people with everyday items," she says, trying to make small talk.

I smile at her but don't add anything to the conversation. "Your total is $12.89," I tell her.

Her smile falters, and she gives me her debit card.

I hand it back to her with a receipt. "Have a nice day."

She turns to leave, then changes her mind, turning back around. "Can you make other kinds of medicine?"

Now I've been blindsided and really don't know what to say. My heart quickens as she stares at me, expecting an answer. "I... maybe? Does the apothecary stock what you're looking for?"

"Not really. I've talked to the owner, and she has a few different supplements for migraines, but none of them even takes the edge off what I deal with. I have a prescription, but it makes me so tired that it's not a great solution."

I am in this position because I put myself here. By helping the young woman with the rash, I have inadvertently caused a stir, and now everyone thinks I'm the town healer.

Should I say no? Part of me *wants* to help. A part that has been buried for such a long time that I forgot she existed.

Can I do this? I'm torn between hope and dread, and I don't know which way to turn.

I make a decision.

"I may be able to help with that, but no promises. Can you come back tomorrow?"

I don't know if it was the right one.

Seven

I'm home and should be preparing dinner since I'm expecting Wendy shortly.

Instead, I'm mixing instant coffee, magnesium, lemon, a small amount of salt and a pinch of sugar. I wonder if this mixture will help with migraines on its own, or if adding a small amount of dark chocolate would increase its efficacy.

It's honestly going to taste terrible, but if it does help, I can order some empty capsules to make it easier to stomach.

I consider again whether I'm changing or just making a huge mistake. I should stay invisible.

Why am I making this difficult? If I don't fade back into obscurity, could everything implode?

I pour myself a glass of wine and take out an empty glass for Wendy. I start my cooking process, following my favorite salmon recipe to the milligram; things are always better when they're measured. I'm not someone who cooks from the heart. It's a regimented process.

I pop the salmon in and continue stirring the risotto so it doesn't burn. The asparagus is already in.

I've set it up perfectly so everything should finish at the same time. I'm starting on the ginger peach galette when there's a knock at the door. I walk over, unlock both deadbolts and let Wendy in.

"Hi! Everything smells great! Thanks for having me." She seems genuinely happy to be here. She hands me a bottle of wine. "Here's my contribution to dinner."

Maisie is so excited to see her that she's practically vibrating with it.

Kicking off her shoes, Wendy sits on the floor. Maisie lies in her lap, happily accepting belly rubs.

Once Maisie is satiated, Wendy curls up on the couch and pulls my blanket over her while she watches me finish cooking.

I'm watching her too, as she takes in the sparseness of my apartment. This isn't the first time she's been here, but we typically hang out at her place or at Root if I'm not working. Her shop is basically my second home, my way of quietly being involved without necessarily being seen.

I can see the wheels turning in her head, trying to puzzle out why I'm the way I am. I'm grateful, both that she doesn't ask the question out loud and that she loves me anyway.

I didn't make it easy for her, but she vaulted over the walls of my emotional fortress regardless.

Our initial meeting took place shortly after I moved to Ashbourne. She had stopped into Sanderson's to pick up a few things and was trying to make small talk. I, of course, wanted no part of it. My lack of participation didn't seem to bother her; she kept right on chatting as if we were already friends.

As she was leaving, I accidentally knocked the "leave a penny, take a penny" container off the counter, and she came back to help me pick up the stray coins. I was irritated and wished she would go away, but she didn't.

I look over at her, and she smiles back.

Part of me has always felt like she somehow saw past the veneer I use to steer people away. She didn't buy it, even from the beginning.

At that time, she was preparing to open Root and would bring me small gifts from the stock: A bottle of essential oils to help with relaxing, a silk hair tie or a nutrient-rich "green juice" that she was excited to have people try.

The oven beeps. The salmon needs a few minutes to rest.

I really tried not to like her. I wanted to huddle at my place, hiding. I thought I could survive on just water, food and terror. But Wendy wasn't having it. It was like she knew what I needed better than I did, and she wasn't going to stop until she was on the inside.

I agreed to help her with finishing touches to get Root off the ground and prepare for opening day. Those hours spent in the empty apothecary, with Wendy chatting as if we'd always been friends, were a salve for the soul that I hadn't realized how much I needed. She slipped through the cracks in my armor, and even if she doesn't know everything about me, she knows more than almost anyone.

I finish prepping dessert and sit next to her, handing her a wine glass. She makes small talk about signing the contract with the vendor of the insomnia tincture and starts discussing her expansion plans for next year. I listen intently until the timer on the stove goes off.

Dinner's ready.

The smell of risotto and salmon is intoxicating, and I realize I'm starving.

Wendy sits down at my small table, and I carry the half-full wine bottle over and set it down for easy refills. Over dinner, Wendy tells me about a guy she met that she's been talking to casually. She's in no rush to get into a relationship, but he seems like a decent human, and she's attracted to him.

Does she see long-term potential there?

She isn't sure. Only time will tell.

I mostly listen; it's what I do best.

Once dinner is done and we've decimated the galette, we go back to the couch and throw on an old movie for background noise.

Wendy looks at me, and I can tell there is something she wants to say, knowing I won't like it.

I take a sip of wine. "What?"

Why am I encouraging this?

"I heard what you did for Shelly yesterday," she begins.

I sigh. "Of course you did. It seems everyone in Ashbourne has at this point." I look down and pick at a piece of fuzz on my shirt. "I don't know why it's such a big deal."

Wendy looks at me and gently says, "You went out of your way to help someone that you could have just dismissed. Everyone is talking about it, not just because it was kind, but because it was impressive. I didn't even know you knew how to make old folk recipes. Where did you learn that?"

I think for a moment. It's sad how little Wendy knows about who I was before I came here. Maybe it's time to open up, just a little. "It wasn't a folk remedy, it's just chemistry."

As the words leave my lips, I cringe.

Now Wendy is looking at me curiously. "What do you mean?"

"Well, apple cider vinegar to restore skin pH, neutralize alkaline irritants and soothe itchy skin. Baking soda neutralizes surface acidity. Aloe also soothes and has anti-inflammatory properties, and tea tree acts as an antiseptic. It's just science."

I move over to the table to refill my glass. To take the edge off and avoid the incredulous look on Wendy's face.

She is still sitting on the couch, her mouth hanging partially open, eyes wide like she's just seen me for the first time. "Leah... what's going on? I've never seen this part of you before."

I clam up and feel the world start to compress, but I breathe through it this time. "I... I don't know if I can talk about my past. I've been running from it for years now."

She stands and walks to my side. "Leah, I'm your best friend," she says, putting her hand over mine. "There isn't anything you can't tell me. Whatever happened, I'm here to listen." This is the first time she's ever overtly asked me to open up. It's the furthest she's ever pushed.

I steady myself and take another sip of wine. Am I going to crack open the door? As risky as I know it is, I can feel in my bones that for the sake of my own humanity, I can no longer fend her off. My revelations will be as much for me as they are for her.

"Our backgrounds are more similar than you'd probably think." I close my eyes as a painful flashback of my facility rips through me. The machinery. The smell of isopropyl alcohol and plastic. The cold metal of the lab benches pressed into my abdomen through my shirt. Things I have tried to push away for years. The memory cuts me to the bone.

Shock registers on Wendy's face as she realizes that I'm going to trust her with information about my background. She didn't expect me to grant her request.

I'm a little shocked myself, and more than slightly terrified, but I push through. "I was in medical research. I have a master's degree in biomedical science and was more than halfway through my PhD in pharmacology before I left. My situation was a lot like what you've described before: burnout and an unbelievable amount of stress. The difference is that my career ended abruptly. I wasn't on the same page with corporate."

I can see Wendy trying to process the information I've just given her. She seems at a loss for words. I don't think she ever thought I wasn't intelligent, but she had no idea quite how educated I really am, and in a field so similar to her own.

"That's incredible!" she says, her face both delighted and sympathetic. "Why on earth did you think you couldn't tell me? You know I've been there. I know that feeling, exactly. If there's anyone in the world who would understand what you've been through, it's me."

"It... just wasn't important," I reply, unsure if telling her even this much was me widening my mistake, making it bigger, giving it depth with no real benefit.

"It *IS* important!" she replies. "And now the way you cook, measuring every ingredient to the microgram, makes so much more sense!" She laughs, but I don't laugh with her.

"Can we talk about something else? I think we've done enough soul searching for tonight," I say wearily. I feel as if I've lost 10 pounds, but there is still a tightness in my chest.

Wendy moves a step closer and hugs me, something she has never attempted before. "Thank you, Leah. Thank you for trusting me with your past. I know it wasn't easy," she says gently.

I reactively tense, but then something inside me gives. The armor that has kept me safe crumbles and I put my arms around her, too. Tears start to form, and I let them fall as I bury my face in her shoulder.

Somehow, I feel better but worse at the same time.

Eight

The rest of the night is calm, as Wendy can sense that what she's learned is all I'm capable of for one day.

She tells me a funny story about a customer who didn't properly read the instructions on a tincture and came back today without eyebrows. I laugh, glad to be past our earlier conversation, at least for now. We finish our wine, and Wendy says goodbye, giving me one more hug on her way out the door.

I don't tense up quite as much this time, and I turn the porch light on for her descent to the driveway.

With Wendy gone, I wash the dirty dishes and put away the leftover galette. I'll probably eat it for lunch tomorrow.

I tidy up, then start my bedtime routine.

Taking Maisie out for the last time tonight, I hear the owl, but no other strange sounds. There's nothing in the darkness but naked trees in the wind, Maisie and me.

Lying in bed, I'm calmer than usual. Something feels different. Between the rash cream, the migraine remedy and my confession to Wendy tonight, something has shifted. At that fork in the road, I made a choice. Several, actually, that are going to impact my life from here on. I still don't know if they were the right ones, but there's a small part of me that feels... quiet inside—isolated from my typical inner turmoil.

I toss and turn only minimally before falling asleep.

I wake the next morning with no memory of dreaming. It's still dark outside, so I check the time. It's 5:30 a.m. I sigh, knowing I'll never get back to sleep.

Getting up, I make coffee and twist myself into a pretzel during yoga. I do an extra half hour this morning, because it keeps my mind on my breath and off my own problems. Putting the leftover galette in the oven to warm it up, I grab my tablet to scan the news.

I'm scanning the headlines, enjoying the quiet peacefulness with coffee in hand, when I come across an interesting one: "New Drug Trial Shows Promising Results in Autoimmune Neurology." As I begin to read the article, my stomach drops.

A team at Novagenix Biotech (NovGen) is reporting early success with a new drug, which is said to regenerate nerve pathways damaged by autoimmune disorders. The compound, derived from the same base molecule as the discontinued NVX-201 therapy, is being hailed as a breakthrough by early investors. Clinical trials begin in the next six months.

Of all the programs for them to resurrect, it had to be that one?

I sit and absorb this information for a minute, then keep scrolling, looking for similar headlines. There are no others that offer a deeper analysis or more context on this program. I run my hands down my face and decide I've had enough internet for today.

Eating the leftover galette is a welcome distraction. There is no meal better than day-old dessert.

When it's gone, I get ready for the day and decide it's time to take Maisie for a real walk, which we haven't done in a while. I grab her leash from the closet and put on a warm winter hat and jacket. Maisie is so excited that she may implode if we don't get outside quickly.

We walk down my street and out to the main one that brings us to town. The air is brisk and cold, but it's nice to be outdoors. Maisie stops constantly, wanting to experience every new smell, tail wagging happily as we make our way.

I haven't decided yet where we're going; we'll see where the day takes us.

We pass Root, and then Sanderson's a few minutes later. We walk by a computer repair place, a Dunkin' Donuts and a new plant shop that recently opened.

At the end of the street, we turn left and start to walk away from the center of town. I don't plan to stray too far, but Maisie's enjoying the walk so much that we keep going until the lake comes into view.

In the summer, it's a busy place. Ashbourne doesn't allow motorboats, but people still go swimming, kayaking, paddleboarding, and just generally soaking up the sun.

At this time of year, the lakeside is empty of tourists and locals alike. It hasn't frozen over enough for ice skating, leaving it mostly abandoned until it's of use again.

Our proximity to the lake reminds me again of my dream from the other night, and I feel unease start to creep in. We're far enough from civilization that if we were to stumble into a bad situation, nobody would hear us. I decide on one quick lap around the lake, and then we will head home.

The top layer of water is frozen over, but it hasn't snowed yet. The ice is beautiful, sparkling against the glare of the morning sunlight. A slight breeze blows through the pines, and their needles make a whispering noise. The air smells fresh, and the crunching of leaves under our feet is therapeutic.

It really does feel good to be out of the house with a sky full of sunshine. I take a deep but cold breath, and let it out slowly, feeling the air prickle my lungs in that way that only happens after late fall.

Some bushes near us start to rustle, and Maisie and I both immediately go on high alert, but it's only a fox looking for breakfast. This settles me, but Maisie doesn't feel the same.

We're about halfway around the lake when the hair on my neck pricks up, and it's not from the cold.

Suddenly, my eyes are drawn toward the tree line. About 30 yards away, I see the sun glint off something shiny, though I can't make out what it is. As fast as I think I see it, it disappears.

I'm unnerved and consider going back, but since we're halfway around, it's the same distance no matter the path. Maisie doesn't seem bothered, so we keep walking.

I'm not panicked, but I am now on alert, and I continuously scan the tree line for anything out of the ordinary. A few minutes pass, and again I see a flash near the edge of the woods, still 30 yards away, as if whatever is moving is moving with us.

Again, it disappears.

I don't know what is out there, but I have the distinct feeling it's tracking us.

We walk faster, but subtly. I don't want to draw attention to the fact that I'm looking for someone in the woods.

My heart rate spikes.

I feel like if we can get out to the road, we may be able to run fast enough to town that we have a chance of outrunning them.

There are about five more minutes of walking to get all the way around the lake. Maisie is still happily walking along as if nothing is wrong, and I'm glad that the glint isn't close enough to us that she's picked up on it.

Keeping my eyes on the tree line, I scan for more signs of someone watching us when Maisie starts barking loudly.

I jump and start to run, but then I look ahead and see that Mina is walking towards us, a dark bag slung over her shoulder. I stop in my tracks, unsure what to do. Everything in me says to turn around and run the other way, but my options are to run into the woods or to run 20 minutes back around the lake.

Mina is in excellent shape. With her long legs, if she wants to, she'll catch me. My gut says Mina isn't a threat, but my head says that everyone is.

With the glint in the woods, I'm feeling more threatened than usual this morning. I decide that my best chance is to find out what Mina is here for and hope it doesn't have to do with my past.

"Hey, Mina!" I call out, trying to sound cheerful and optimistic, the way a normal human would while walking their dog on a beautiful morning in such a gorgeous location.

"Good morning, Leah! How are you?" she responds with a smile. "Chilly this morning, isn't it?"

Okay, so far, so good.

My initial impression is that it's possible she's out for a morning walk herself. I smile at her, "I'm doing well, thanks! I decided to take my dog for a nice walk today; it's been a while since the weather has been so chilly. This is Maisie!" I say, gesturing toward her. Maisie's tail wags as Mina draws closer and stops to chat.

"Oh, hi, Maisie!" Mina says, crouching down to give Maisie a quick pat. "What a pretty girl you are!"

I'm still on edge, but the world hasn't closed in around me. Maisie seems to like Mina, and so far, it just seems like a coincidence that we've bumped into her. "Are you out for a walk too?" I ask.

She holds up the bag she's carrying. "Actually, one of my hobbies is photography. I especially love taking nature photos. I'm an amateur, but I couldn't pass up the chance to come out here while I'm visiting. Isn't it beautiful?"

She takes her camera out of her pack and shows me a few photos she's snapped this morning. She's actually pretty good for a beginner.

"Wow, Mina, these are gorgeous!" I hear myself saying. Then something occurs to me. "Have you been in this general area all morning?"

"Yes, pretty much," she replies, while putting her camera back in her pack. She points behind me. "I started over that way, maybe a mile in, and I've been working my way back toward the street for the last hour or so. I was just finishing up when I saw you two. Maybe we could walk back together?"

I breathe a huge sigh of relief.

What I saw glinting in the woods must have been a reflection from the sun on Mina's camera lens. I am so glad we ran into her, so I didn't spend the rest of the day spiraling, cocooned in my own terror. "Sure, that sounds great," I tell her.

We start to walk back toward the road. Out of the corner of my eye, I think I see a quick flash, but by the time I look in that direction, it's gone.

I shrug it off.

It must have been a trick of the light.

But if that's the case, why does my chest still hurt?

Nine

We make it back to the road within a few minutes.

Walking together, we've fallen into a rhythm that feels natural, even safe.

I know that something has begun to change in me because I want to know Mina better. I don't want to make small talk; I want to know more about her.

Do I genuinely have the capacity to make friends?

"So, what do you do when you're not back home visiting Ashbourne?" I ask.

She replies naturally, as if it's a question she is asked all the time. "I work in crisis management. Essentially, I help plan for emergencies and operational risks. It's a professional way of saying I make sure everyone else is prepared for inevitable mistakes."

"That sounds like an interesting career," I counter.

Mina glances at me as she replies, "Sure, it's fine. It pays the bills, but it's not rocket science. Mostly it's understanding what people do without supervision, and how small things that seem insignificant can turn into huge mistakes." She runs her fingers through her hair to push back the few strands that have fallen into her eyes.

I decide that since she's told me this much, I may as well keep going. I'm enjoying learning about her life. "Where do you manage these crises from?" I ask.

She smiles slightly. "I live near Boston most of the time, but I travel a lot. My work brings me all over the country."

I pause, remembering what it was like to have an interesting life. I may be in my own head a moment too long, because Mina picks the conversation back up. I hope I didn't make it awkward. I have a way of doing that lately.

"What about you?"

I cast my eyes downward, ashamed to have to tell her how I earn my living. "I work at Sanderson's," I say dryly. "It's not engaging or particularly challenging, but it keeps a roof over my head."

Now I'm regretting having started this line of conversation. I want to crawl into a hole somewhere and disappear.

Mina's demeanor changes as she senses my discomfort in having told her what I do for a living. "So your job isn't flashy, so what? If it keeps you warm in the winter and food on your table, then I think you're doing just fine. It's practical. There are a lot of people I know who could use a dose of that."

I'm grateful that Mina doesn't try to dig, to unearth information I'm not able or willing to give.

I decide I'm going to be the one who does that. "So, you grew up here?" I ask.

She stiffens slightly but then relaxes again as if she knew the question would come up eventually. "Yes," she says softly. "My family moved here in elementary school." She doesn't add more context.

I pry just a little based on my conversation with Wendy at lunch the other day. "Do you know Wendy Farrow? She runs Root, the pharmacy on Archer Street in town."

She sighs and runs her fingers through her hair again, this time seemingly out of nervousness. Hesitating for a beat, she resigns herself to telling her story. "Yes, I know Wendy. We went to school together for 10 years. She was one of the smart, popular girls. We were both friends with Megan, but she and I never really clicked. I was skinny, tall and just generally plain and awkward. She didn't so much *bully* me as pretend I didn't exist."

I can see the pain on her face as she recalls her childhood memories. "I know it was years ago, but I generally just avoid Root when I'm back in town. It's a 'me' problem, I'm sure she doesn't even remember it."

I feel a pang of sadness for Mina. The tightly wrapped plaster I've sealed around my heart is failing me. The more she tells me, the more I want to know. "I'm so sorry, Mina. That sounds awful. I don't think that's just a 'you' problem. Have you ever considered telling Wendy how she made you feel? She's pretty much my only friend these days, and I can't see her being anything other than sorry about how she treated you in school."

Mina looks ashamed, and I feel like I've caught her in a vulnerable position. I get the feeling it's something she is not used to, talking about her past. "I couldn't," she says. "There are some things that are better just left in the past."

I nod, agreeing with her. If anyone understands that much, it's me. Then something occurs to me. "Have you always gone by 'Mina'? I had told Wendy about you picking me up on the way home from the party on Saturday, and she didn't recognize the name."

There's a sad smile on her face. "No, Mina is a nickname, but I legally changed it about 10 years ago. Through school, I was Willa, short for Wilhelmina. It's almost like even my parents didn't like me much. When I went away to college, I told everyone my name was Mina, and my life drastically improved from there. I'm sure it wasn't my name that changed my life, but Mina felt more grown-up and just all-around the 'me' I wanted to be. It allowed me to step outside the box of expectations that others had built for me. The rest is pretty much history."

Well, another mystery solved. I have no doubt that when I ask Wendy about "Willa," she will at least know the name and who Mina was during their years growing up here. I'm so glad I asked. I decide to continue questioning her. "How often do you come home to visit? Your parents still live here?"

Between the very personal information she's just shared with me and this new line of questioning, she looks slightly uncomfortable but takes a breath and brightens as if she's trying not to show it. "I come back home every few months to check on them. They were older when I was born, so they're retired now, and I don't have any siblings. I'll typically stay for a week or so to make sure that everything is in order. I can do most of my job remotely, so I don't burn up vacation time when I'm here."

Mina has shared a lot with me, and I don't want to make her uncomfortable, but I feel like I've opened gates that have been sealed for such a long time that I don't want to stop learning about her. "And how about at home? Are you married? Any kids?"

She now looks like a deer in headlights. Then she chuckles, her shoulders relaxing. "Now you sound just like my parents. Every time I come back, I get the third degree about my personal life."

I wince. "Sorry, I didn't mean to get too personal. It's just been weirdly comfortable talking to you."

This time, a hearty laugh escapes. "It's fine, I really don't mind. I'm just not used to answering to anyone other than Mom and Dad: no husband, no kids, no real ties to anyone but friends. I think a lot of that is because I travel so often. I haven't exactly been looking to meet someone."

I take a closer look at Mina. She's beautiful, in a really unique way. Her hazel eyes border on green, with gold starbursts at their centers. Standing next to her, I'd definitely place her at about 5'9". She's tall in that effortless supermodel way. I know she described herself as skinny and awkward as a kid, but as an adult, she's grown into her looks.

I surmise that if she hasn't met someone, it's not because of a lack of options.

We're back in town now, and our walk slows to a stop as I sense we're about to part ways.

Standing in front of Sanderson's, we have a brief moment of awkwardness as neither of us seems sure how to say goodbye after such a chance meeting in the woods.

It's that stage of a relationship where you aren't quite friends and don't know whether to say 'Let's hang out later' or just 'Okay, see you around.'

Mina breaks the silence. "Do you walk in the woods often? Maybe I'll see you there again sometime."

It's an interesting bridge between the two options I had outlined, and I'm grateful that she took charge of this part of the conversation. "I haven't been lately; it's been pretty cold. See you around town, maybe?"

I don't want to tell her that the feeling of being watched in the woods has stuck with me, and I may not go back until spring, when there will be other people around.

A look of relief quickly flashes across her face, and then it's gone. "Sounds good!" she smiles. "See you around!" She walks off in the direction of the black sedan she drove me home in the other night.

Weird.

Did she want to walk so badly that she left her car in town and hauled her camera equipment on foot into the woods? It seems like an odd choice, but I still don't know her very well.

Maybe she just really likes to walk.

Maisie and I continue walking back to my apartment. The extra few minutes give me time to process everything that happened this morning.

I'm almost sure that what I saw in the woods was Mina's camera. It makes logical sense; she was there at the same time and moving in the same direction, so of course the glint I was seeing was moving at the same pace we were. And the movement I saw at the very end of the walk, I didn't even actually see. It could have been the fox, still hunting for breakfast.

We're approaching my house now, and I'm glad to be home. There seems to never be a dull moment in my otherwise very dull life.

Just as I'm having this thought, I hear and feel a *crunch* under my feet and notice some broken glass near my car, parked in front of the house.

My front tire is flat.

Ten

I get Maisie in the house, then go back out to inspect my tire.

Ugh, it's going to cost me money I don't really have to fix.

It's not even the tire I filled the other day.

I try to think back to when I parked after my lunch with Wendy. It's possible that I ran over the glass, which caused the flat, but I really don't remember any glass being there.

It's strewn halfway down the length of the vehicle, so if I had run it over the other day, I would have stepped on it when I got out.

I sigh heavily.

I feel like I'm doing that a lot more these days.

I go back inside and call the local repair shop. The owner's name is Pete, and he's a nice enough guy, but he always hits on me and it gives me the creeps.

"Pete's Auto Repair!" A shrill voice chirps out. It's his administrative assistant, Donna. She's loud and a little too inquisitive for me, but overall, she's friendly and warm. She has the perfect personality for customer service.

"Hi, Donna," I greet her. "How are you? It's Leah Mercer over on Rowan Street." They know me because I always have my car at the shop for one thing or another.

"Leah, honey, how are you?" Donna says warmly. "What can we do for you?"

"I've been better, Donna," I reply. "I've got a flat tire. I was hoping Pete was around today to tow it to the shop."

"Give me just a minute, hon. I'll check with him and see when he can get over there."

An hour later, Pete is in front of my house, loading my car onto his flatbed tow truck. He's wearing his blue mechanic's uniform with his name embroidered on it. That's about where the comparison to any mechanic you've ever met ends.

He's always squeaky clean.

And don't get me wrong, I get why mechanics always have stained hands and clothes. It's literally their job. But Pete must go through five uniforms a day. He always looks spic-and-span. If he weren't in uniform, you'd mistake him for a car salesman. His hair is always shiny and styled, his hands are free of grease, and he always smells of cologne. I've never watched him work, but he must wear gloves and a raincoat. There is no other way he could stay as clean as he does.

He flashes me a pearly white smile as he leans on his fender while winching my car up. "What's new, Leah? How is life treating you? Seeing anyone?"

I smile artificially. Pete is a great mechanic, but he makes me uncomfortable, just like anyone who notices me more than in passing. "I've been better, Pete," I echo what I told Donna earlier. "Not having a car in winter, even for a few days, isn't ideal." I ignore the other questions.

"I'll get this fixed up for you in no time. No worries, Leah." He uses my name too often, like maybe it makes us closer, more personal.

"Thank you. Any idea what this will run me?" I'm concerned about how far back this will set me financially.

"Well, Leah, I'll see what I can do. If I can find a tire in the scrapyard that's the right size and not too worn, it shouldn't be more than around $100. If I can't and you need a new set, you're looking at $400–500." He finishes pulling my car up onto the tow truck, then wipes his hands with baby wipes and dries them on a towel from the cab.

"I'll have Donna call you this afternoon to let you know the actual damage."

"Thank you, Pete. I appreciate you getting out here so fast." I'll hold my breath until I hear from Donna later about which way it's going to go.

When I get back inside, I check the time and see that it's already after one o'clock. Groaning, I realize I have to be at work for two today, and I'm working until close tonight.

I take a quick shower and eat the fastest lunch possible, and then I'm out the door and walking.

With no car, I'll have to walk home tonight in the dark again. Maybe I'll call Wendy and see if she can bring me home. The walk the other night had me on edge, so if I can avoid this one, I will.

Today is Tuesday, so the store will be busy with locals running in and out for staples to make their dinners and breakfasts during the week.

By 5 p.m., Carla is here with Lilly, though Carla is engaged in conversation with some other regulars in the sitting area. Lilly is curled up reading a book with a blanket over her lap.

Brad also shows up at five, though he's only here until eight tonight, so at least I only have a few hours of avoiding him to look forward to. "Hi, Brad," I greet him.

He looks shocked that I said hello for the first time in two years. "Good evening, Leah. How are you? Busy today?"

"I'm fine, thanks, Brad. Yeah, it's been steady so far."

He ducks out back to the break room to put away his jacket, and I stay at the register, checking people out as they come in, weave through the store and then leave with their purchases. Everything is pretty normal; a small spill in aisle 2, someone asking if we have more stock out back (we don't).

Then Kayla walks in to pick up her migraine remedy.

My heart quickens. I really don't want to draw attention to myself, so I ask Brad to cover the register, and I walk her to the back of the store.

I hand her the bottle, tell her what's in it and warn her that it's going to taste terrible. I also give her instructions on the proper quantity and ask her to let me know if it works. If it does, I can order capsules and fill them so that it's not quite so terrible to take.

She thanks me profusely and tries to pay me. I decline and tell her that if it works for her and she needs a bigger batch, we can work out the details then.

She leaves, practically skipping out the door.

It seems as if my fears about being the center of attention tonight are absolved.

As I head back toward the counter, I see a shadow in my peripheral vision as Carla steps out from behind a dry-goods case.

"What was that about?" she asks, seemingly bristling with agitation. "What did you give her?"

"Oh, it was nothing, Carla. Just a migraine remedy she asked me to make for her. Not a big deal." I shrug and turn toward the counter.

Carla grasps my sleeve so I can't walk away. "Not a big deal?" She is now incensed, and her eyes are full of unshed tears, her finger pointed in my face. "You could hurt someone, KILL someone by mixing a homemade remedy at the wrong dosage. What on earth are you thinking? Do you have ANY moral code whatsoever?"

I'm stunned into silence. Carla's words hit me deeply, and I don't know what to say or do next, so I just stand there, staring at her, mouth hanging open. I can't even stutter out a confused apology for my perceived wrongdoings.

My complete confusion seems to cut through Carla's annoyance, and she realizes that she's just screamed at me in earshot of a dozen people. She backs away from me, then grabs Lilly and storms out the front doors.

Brad comes over to check on me. "Are you okay, Leah? What on earth happened?"

"Honestly, I have no idea. Remember the woman who was here yesterday, asking me about a migraine remedy? She came to pick it up, and Carla completely lost it on me. I don't know why she got so upset. I was just trying to help. Do you mind if I take a quick five out back?"

Brad tells me to take as much time as I need, and I slink out back to cry into some bunched-up paper towels as quietly as possible. I'm not much of a crier, but this was a jolt that my nervous system isn't used to. I grab my phone out of my bag and call Wendy. It goes to voicemail.

"Hi, Wendy, I'm calling because I was hoping you might be able to give me a lift home tonight when Sanderson's closes. I got a flat this morning, so my car is at Pete's shop. I would really appreciate it if you're available. Give me a quick call back and let me know."

Wendy calls back in under a minute and tells me she's closing tonight but can pick me up after. Root also closes at nine, so I should only have to wait a short time.

The rest of my shift is thankfully uneventful. Brad leaves at eight, and Bill pokes his head out to check on me. The rush has slowed down, so I'm just trying to pass the time until my shift is over. I'm trying to focus on tidying the counter area for closing, but I can't get what happened with Carla out of my head.

Do you have *any* moral code whatsoever?

"How's it going out here?" Bill asks.

Without warning, I start to tear up again. I hate my emotions being visible on my face, so now I'm both angry and confused.

Bill, looking concerned, comes out to the counter. "What happened? What's wrong, Leah?"

My eyes are turned down toward the floor, and I can't face him. I don't like people looking at me to begin with, but especially when I don't have full control of my emotions.

I decide to be honest with him. "There was an issue with Carla tonight. I don't understand why she lashed out at me, and now I'm trying to mend my bruised ego while also figuring out what made her so angry." I give him the run-down of what happened, hoping maybe he has more insight than I do.

Bill is sympathetic but just as confused as I am. He tries to make me feel better by letting me choose where the "bats and moon" painting will be hung in the shop.

Strangely, it does make me feel a bit better.

It's finally time to close up, and I'm still upset and working through all the reasons I can think of that would cause Carla to lash out, but I keep coming up empty. I turn out the lights, say goodnight to Bill and lock the door behind me. I'm sitting on a bench outside, waiting for Wendy, when Carla appears out of nowhere. I stand up and back away, unsure what she's here for.

"Hi, Leah," she says wearily. "I'm here to apologize. I'm truly sorry that I reacted the way I did earlier." She looks up, as if the reason she exploded might be written in the sky. "I don't have a great explanation, but I wanted to try and make you understand. When Lilly was born, she was sick. What the doctors did solved one problem but created many more. I always think that someone should have stopped it. Seeing you and these 'remedies' the last few days has had me on edge. I know that's not your fault." After a quick pause, she adds, "I've been a little under the weather this week, and it's been stressful. I'm sorry."

She doesn't meet my eyes during the apology, and she sounds exhausted. There's a strange tone to her voice that doesn't make sense to me, but I nod, just wanting this moment to end.

"It's okay, Carla. I'm sorry to have triggered you. I didn't know about Lilly's past. I can't imagine how hard that must have been for you."

She finally looks at me, and she seems strangely hurt, almost like I had slapped her. "Thanks, Leah."

Her tone sounds flat.

At that moment, Wendy pulls up and honks. She smiles and rolls down the window. "Hi, Carla! How have you been? How's Lilly?" She doesn't realize that she has, thankfully, just broken up a tense conversation.

Eleven

I practically leap into the car, saying a rushed goodbye to Carla as I slam the door on that exchange.

I have never been so happy to be picked up. I've never been more grateful to have asked Wendy for a ride before.

"What's up?" Wendy asks. "How was your day?" She puts the car in gear, and we start toward my house.

I laugh ironically, "Oh, it's been an interesting one. I thought I was being followed this morning in the woods, then I got home to a flat tire, and then Carla screamed at me while I was working. I'm honestly very glad this day is over." I press the seat-warmer button, then sink into the chair as the heat kicks in.

Wendy's eyes go wide. "Carla *yelled* at you? What happened? I can't even picture what you could have done to cause that!" I can see the wheels in Wendy's head turning as she's trying to puzzle out this very bizarre turn of events.

I pause, as much from exhaustion as from not wanting to replay the scene just yet. "Long story short, I made another remedy for someone, Carla caught on even though I was trying to be private, and then she blew up at me in front of a store full of customers. She was just here apologizing to me for the way she handled herself earlier. I still don't really understand, but apparently something happened when Lilly was young, and now she's on edge with people taking... medicine? Holistic medicine? Like I said, I'm still not sure why she was so upset. But she did apologize, even if her vibe was weird. It's Carla, so strange interactions are normal, I guess."

Wendy whistles and glances at me. "You really have had a day, haven't you? That's so weird. I don't get it either. At least she came back to apologize."

We're pulling up to my house now, and though we sit for a minute finishing the conversation, I don't invite her in, and she doesn't ask.

"Yeah," I say. "It has been a day. I can't wait to get into my sweats and just lie in bed, comatose. Thanks for picking me up, I hate walking at night even though it's not very far."

"No problem at all. Anytime. I was glad to get the scoop on Carla at least today. Are you working tomorrow?"

"Thankfully no," I tell her. My plan for tomorrow is to veg on the couch, read or maybe watch a movie. I don't want to see another person.

In that moment, my phone rings.

"Hey, Leah! It's Pete. Sorry to call so late, but it's been a busy day. Good news! I did have a tire that will fit your car, so I'll get that on and wrapped up by tomorrow afternoon. Can you come pick it up around three?"

I ask Pete to hold on a second and whisper to Wendy, "Are you working tomorrow? Can you take me to Pete's to pick up my car in the afternoon?"

She says she's working in the morning but has the afternoon off, so it's no problem.

"Hey, Pete? Yeah, thanks for waiting. I can be there. I really appreciate it."

So much for not seeing another person tomorrow.

I kick my shoes off and collapse on the couch. Maisie is doing her happy dance, tail wagging, ecstatic to see me.

She decides she can't wait another minute for love, so she starts licking my face.

I am so emotionally exhausted that I can't even bring myself to sit on the floor with her. I pet her from my spot on the couch, hoping it will calm her enough that I can just exist for a minute. She accepts this compromise and happily takes my attention.

Finally, she's had enough. When she realizes dinner isn't incoming yet, she lopes off to nap in her very comfy dog bed.

I lie on the couch, trying to process everything that happened today. My and Maisie's walk, Mina, my tire, Carla. It's been a day that I wouldn't have had the ability to get through even two weeks ago. So many issues, people and distractions. All the events keep spinning around in my mind like a washing machine with a broken spin cycle.

Can I trust Mina? Did I really run over the broken glass and not notice? Was Carla's apology as weird as it seemed to me?

I'm tired. Physically and mentally.

I wake on the couch hours later, then go to the bathroom before stumbling to bed.

Though I fall asleep again easily afterward, a dream follows me back into my subconscious depths.

I'm standing on a small platform, my back against tall wooden posts, like small trees that have been roughly cut just for this purpose.

There are people all around the circular dais, milling about with faces turned away from me, waiting for something. The energy is charged, electric excitement in the air.

I try to step down, but notice my wrists and ankles are bound with twine.

A long, stiff black dress with a high collar itches against my skin.

I look back to the crowd, and they're now facing me. They look angry, eyebrows knitted together, sternly looking on.

I see faces I recognize: Brad, Shelly, the balding man from the apartment building, customers of Sanderson's. They begin to screech loud, enraged accusations at me about my past.

I see Wendy and Bill in the very back, trying to push people aside to reach me, but their path is continually blocked.

Mina is in the middle. Not shouting, just watching.

Finally, a man I've never seen before steps to the front.

"*Burn, bitch,*" he says, loudly but calmly.

He strikes a match and bends down to light the hay and wood kindling at my feet.

Twelve

I wake with a start, beads of sweat decorating my forehead.

Blinking against the bright light coming in through the living room windows, I realize it's nearly nine o'clock.

I've slept almost ten hours straight.

Sitting up, my mind briefly returns to the nightmare. I scratch the back of my neck, remembering the high, itchy collar. My hands tremble as I pull back the covers.

Maisie is still snoring softly, not the slightest bit upset that she missed dinner.

I stretch my arms over my head. The couch is comfortable, but I have a few aches today from the hours I spent sleeping on it. I should be able to stretch them out during yoga this morning.

Getting out of bed, I'm still disoriented. I shiver, then layer a sweater over my pajamas before going to the kitchen to start the coffee pot.

After my usual morning routine of breakfast and news headlines, I decide that Maisie deserves another walk today. This time, we stick close to the house, keeping it to a short half hour. She's happy, and I'm much calmer than yesterday.

Again, I think about how much getting a good night's sleep really shifts your mood.

At eleven o'clock, I decide I'm going to walk to Root a bit early. Wendy is off at noon, but it's not the first time I've gone there to kill an hour or two.

The walk to town is relaxing, and my yoga session helped stretch out my back pain from the couch.

Overall, I feel good this morning. Yesterday was hectic, but at least it's over now. Picking up my car later will be the last thing I need to resolve everything.

I walk into Root and hear the "ding!" of the doorbell, which alerts Wendy to customers entering or exiting the store. I smell lavender, sage and lemongrass and am transported back to Nan's house.

My nan is an unusual woman. She's a natural healer who believes that rocks and minerals have special healing abilities and that many remedies can be made from herbs and household items.

In some ways, she isn't wrong. My own love of science grew, not in spite of, but because of her beliefs.

Growing up, I learned that lavender could help you sleep and that ashwagandha could lower stress. As I got older, I wanted to know *why* these remedies worked. So, I started studying.

I knew in middle school that I wanted to work in some facet of science. Nan's remedies were the catalyst for my future career, and I took it as far as I could go. I think back again to my dream of her the other night: *Find your way home, and you will find your way forward.* There is nothing I wish for more, but home no longer exists for me.

"Hi, Leah!" Wendy breaks the spell of my musings, and I'm brought back to the present. "You're early! Are you planning to hang out for a bit?" She's checking out a customer in the pharmacy.

I nod, signaling that I'll be here when she's done.

Roots and Remedies is set up so that about two-thirds of the space is dedicated to holistic remedies, crystals, herbal teas, organic goods, house plants and locally made gifts. The remaining third of the store is a pharmacy counter with a small meeting room for confidential advice or vaccine administration. It's the busier side of Wendy's business and brings in the majority of her income, despite its smaller footprint.

Wendy's story is similar to my own, but she loves healing people. She will always recommend over-the-counter products to fix a problem before resorting to pharmaceuticals.

If there's a way to help without drugs, she'll find it. She stocks a homeopathic cure for just about any issue you can think of, and she will make sure you've tried everything. She even gives out samples for people to test before buying.

Wendy finishes up with her customer and walks over. "What's up? Just decided to stop by early?" She gives me a quick hug.

I tense up, closing my eyes. When I open them, she's already walking back toward the shop counter.

"Want to help me make these gift baskets? I think they're going to sell well for the holidays!" She grabs a basket and starts loading it with different products: hand cream, scented candles and lavender room spray. She has a bin of items she's using to make the baskets from. Once they're full, she wraps them in plastic and shrinks them with a hair dryer to keep everything contained.

"Sure!" I laugh. "I don't mind being free labor." I smile at her, grateful to have someone like Wendy in my life. She's grounded, funny, intelligent and kind.

She elbows me playfully. "Consider it payback for me being your chauffeur. What time am I dropping you off at the shop?"

"Three o'clock," I say. "I know you get out at noon, so I guess I'm tagging along for whatever errands you have to run today." I didn't think about that when I asked her yesterday.

Her brow furrows. "I don't think you want to come to my doctor's appointment. It's at twelve thirty. You can sit in the car, if you want to?" She looks like she feels bad for having prior plans.

"No, it's okay. I'll just hang out in town until you're back. It's not a big deal." Though I am wondering what I'm going to do in town for an hour in winter.

I'll figure it out.

"Are you sure?" she asks. "I feel bad, I didn't realize it was going to be so late in the afternoon." I know she doesn't want to leave me, given how paranoid I typically am about everything.

"Yes, I'll be fine. There's a small plant shop that just opened near Sanderson's that I've been meaning to take a peek in, so maybe I'll browse in there for a bit."

"Hey! I sell plants!" she says, feigning shock that I might spend my hard-earned money elsewhere. "Kidding, obviously. I'll call you when I'm on the way back."

Thirteen

I'm walking around the store "Plant Envy," thinking about how I could have been curled up on the couch, half-conscious, all day today if things had gone differently. But here I am, browsing an overpriced plant store that will be gone in six months, knowing I can't even afford a clipping. I'm grateful that my tire is only going to run me about $100, but it's still coming out of my very meager savings account.

My mind wanders briefly back to what it was like to go out for a fancy dinner, buy a new pair of shoes or splurge on a totally unnecessary perfume, just because I could. I was never rich, but I was comfortable. I had a nice apartment, a newer car and an enviable savings account. The savings have dwindled to near nothing, and I'm not really sure what I'm going to do when it eventually runs out.

"Good afternoon, anything I can help you find?"

I jump and turn in the direction of a woman's voice.

She's smiling at me with too-white teeth. They're a shade so bright they make the whites of her eyes appear yellowish.

It's uncanny.

"Oh, no, thank you. I'm just browsing." I feel like I have to explain why I'm here when I'm not actually looking for something. "I saw you opened recently and just wanted to see what this place was about."

She smiles too big, and it doesn't seem genuine. "Oh, that's great! Did you see our ad in the paper or hear the one on the radio? See any flyers? I'm trying to get a feel for what advertisement is working, so it would be helpful to know."

I'm uncomfortable and don't want to talk to her. "No, I just work nearby and have seen this place in passing."

Her smile falters briefly, then she picks it back up. "Oh, that's great! Where do you work?"

I really don't want to tell her, but I feel cornered now. "Sanderson's General Store." I realize that since it's a weekday afternoon, and this place is completely dead, I'm not going to escape a conversation with her unless I leave. "I actually have to be at work shortly. It was nice chatting with you."

She looks at me strangely, probably because I'm dressed casually and don't look like I'm going to work. But she smiles her too-white smile that reflects the fluorescent lights and says, "Thanks for stopping in! Come back anytime!"

I move to leave, and as I'm opening the door, I glance back over my shoulder. She's still looking at me, so I give her an awkward wave as the door shuts behind me.

With nowhere else to be and 45 minutes until Wendy will be back, I head over to Sanderson's, since at least I know Bill will be glad to see me. I walk through the door and see that Brianna and Brad are working this afternoon.

Brad comes over, standing too close to me. "Hey, Leah! What are you doing here today? You're not working, are you? Bill never schedules three of us at a time."

"Hi, Brad. No, I'm just in the area waiting for Wendy to get back from a doctor's appointment. I've got nothing going on, so I thought I'd stop in." I realize how pathetic I sound and laugh uncomfortably.

He gives me a look that's half pity and half amusement. "Bill's out back," he says with a little snort-laugh.

I flush and move past him, greeting Brianna on the way. She's nice enough. Keeps to herself, mostly. She reminds me a little of myself, except more embarrassed and less distrustful.

Bill is doing exactly what you'd expect. He just finished a painting of a forest that, from a distance, looks a little like a Picasso, but the closer you get, the more you realize it's just really bad.

He's looking at two different canvases now, trying to choose between a field of flowers and a dog standing on its hind legs, filling the gas tank of a car.

"Hey, Bill, how's it going?" I say, sitting down at the table across from him.

He looks up. He hadn't noticed me come in. "What are you doing here, kiddo? You're not scheduled today." He looks down again at the canvases as if the fate of the world rests on this decision.

"Just hanging out," I say. "Waiting for Wendy to give me a lift to pick up my car." I had told him yesterday my tale of woe about having to walk to work. "What are you up to?" As if I didn't know.

"Oh, nothing much. Just trying to decide which one of these to do next. The flowers are kind of plain, and the dog is a little weird, don't ya think?" He shakes his head as if neither is a good option. "How much time are you trying to kill?"

"Not too long, I have about 45 minutes until she's back. I went into that bougie plant shop that opened a few doors down, and it was too rich for my blood. I don't have that kind of cash for non-necessities."

Bill looks up again, his gaze soft. He starts to speak, then shakes his head and looks back down.

"What?" I ask.

He glances back up at me. "What are you doing working here, earning next to nothing, Leah? You're a smart girl; you could get a job doing damn near anything you wanted, and you waste your days away at the store. Don't get me wrong, I like having you. You're a great worker, and I consider you a friend, but you're destined for more than this."

I freeze. Bill has never asked me anything like this. I sense that he isn't trying to pry, necessarily. He's trying to give me the confidence boost I need to do something else. He has no idea why I stay.

"There are a lot of reasons, Bill," I say quietly. "This is where I have to be."

He continues looking at me, searching my face for some semblance of an answer, but he doesn't find one.

He nods and then turns back to his choices. "I guess I'll go with the dog," he says.

Wendy picks me up at 1:00, and we still have a couple of hours to kill before picking up my car.

We decide to grab a quick bite at the diner and then window shop for a while.

It's nice to be out with Wendy. I'm always more comfortable when she's by my side. Maybe it's a "power in numbers" sort of thing, but I feel safer with her. Like nothing bad could possibly happen as long as we're together.

We're walking back toward Wendy's car when I hear a familiar voice.

"Hello, dear, how are you?" It's Carla, wearing a wide smile. She then focuses on Wendy. "Hi, Wendy, how have you been?"

Wendy flashes her perfect, warm, Wendy smile and starts up a conversation. "I'm doing great, Carla, how are you? Is Lilly still doing well in school? I know she started an instrument, right? What was it... the violin? Oh, that's wonderful, I'm glad she's liking it so far."

I like that when we're together, Wendy will gladly dominate the conversation with anyone who wants to chat. It leaves me to fade into the background and exist without a spotlight or any scrutiny from other people.

I watch Carla, animatedly telling Wendy about Lilly's weekly music lessons. I study her for a moment. Her clothes, with all the large, hand-sewn pockets, are baggy and misshapen.

Would it not be easier to carry a small purse so she doesn't have to search through multiple pockets for whatever she needs?

I know Carla is odd, but the more I watch her happily chatting away, the more I start to feel bad for what she was handed in life. I've never heard anything about Lilly's father, so I assume that she's a single mom. I don't know what she does for work, but she's always at either Sanderson's or Root. I have no idea how she supports herself and her child.

Lilly is a great kid, but it must be tough having a child with a disability. She's not the little girl who will ever prance across a stage in a bumblebee costume to "I'm a Little Teapot," nor is she the kid practicing a gymnastics routine in their living room. It must be hard for Lilly, too, knowing the other kids have different capabilities than she does. I'm glad that she's found an instrument she likes. In music, she's on even ground with everybody else.

Suddenly, I realize the talking has stopped, and both Carla and Wendy are looking at me as if expecting an answer. I can't tell them that I was deeply analyzing Carla's life and that I hadn't been paying attention. I decide I'll try and wing it. "Oh, yeah, of course," I answer.

Wendy snort-laughs, and Carla looks mildly offended.

"You were completely zoned out, weren't you?" Wendy says.

I flush and cast my eyes downward, feeling completely foolish. "Yes, I was," I reply.

Wendy lets out a belly laugh and then looks at me fondly. "I don't know anyone else who can stand right in the middle of a conversation and not hear a single word. How do you get so completely lost in your own head?"

I smile now, glad that Wendy is at least able to make light of the situation, so I don't just look like a complete jerk in front of Carla.

Wendy repeats the question. "What happened with your tire?"

"Oh," I smile. "Yeah, totally didn't hear that question. It was flat when I got home from a walk yesterday morning. There was glass all around. I must have run it over when I came home the night before."

Carla nods and frowns, as if I had just said I ran over my cat. Maybe she had stopped listening, too?

Wendy looks at her watch. "Well, Carla, we really need to get going. I have to get Leah over to Pete's to pick her car up at three. It was so nice running into you. Please tell Lilly I said hello!"

I give Carla an awkward wave and a "Bye," and walk over to Wendy's car.

"You are such a goober," Wendy says once we're inside.

"Gee, I'm sorry. We can't all be perfect community socialites like you are."

I'm not angry at Wendy's comment; she's right. I never have any idea what to say to people. I was never popular in school and maintained only a few friendships. Back then, it wasn't out of fear.

I was just working on more important things.

Fourteen

We pull up to Pete's shop, and Wendy asks me if I want her to come in with me.

I do. Donna and Pete both make me uncomfortable, though in different ways. Having Wendy there as a buffer sounds like a great idea.

We walk into the small office that's in front of the shop and are greeted by Donna. Her eighties hairstyle and wardrobe seem colorful and almost flashy in the dingy little room.

"Hi, girls, how are you today? Here to pick up your car, Leah? I've got the paperwork and keys right here; that will be $97.44." She looks at Wendy. "How is your shop going, hon? Busy these days? I only get over there when I need something from the pharmacy, and it's never when I have time to browse."

Wendy starts chatting about the business, about her hopes for the upcoming holiday season, and about the weather.

I envy her conversational skills, but I also know I don't want the attention that comes with them.

I take five twenty-dollar bills out of my purse and hand them to Donna. If I can avoid paying with a debit or credit card, I will.

Donna sighs subtly, as if this is the last thing she wanted to have to deal with today. "We don't take a lot of cash these days, hon. You don't have a card?"

"Not on me," I lie. I don't ever leave home without it, but I don't want to use it.

"Ugh, okay. Let me go get Pete and see if he has change." She gets up from the desk, and I can see she must not leave it much, because she's wearing fuzzy pink slippers. She's back a minute later with Pete, who looks like he just stepped off a movie set. His hair is perfectly in place, and his uniform is spotless.

"Good afternoon, ladies, how are you today?" Pete says, flashing a movie-star smile at us. "I hear you need change? We don't typically take cash, but I can, of course, make an exception for you, Leah." He winks at me as he pulls his wallet out of his pocket. As he opens it, his license falls out and slides to a stop at my feet.

I bend down to pick it up and notice that the name on his license isn't Peter or Pietro, but "Walter."

I feel distinct yet familiar distrust rising in me. Pete already made me nervous; now I don't even know his actual name. The garage is literally called "Pete's Garage."

Pete, or Walter, sees me looking at the name on his license, and suddenly he laughs. "Checking out my deets, huh, Leah?"

I look up at him, a wary look on my face. "Walter?" I use his name as a question.

He laughs again. "Yeah, my parents named me Walter, and I always hated it. There was a show on TV that I liked as a kid, and the boy's name was Pete. I liked it so much I started telling people my name was Pete, and it stuck. Now, here I am, 30 years later, and everyone knows me as Pete. Only the doctor and my parents call me by my given name."

Looking over at Donna, she's smiling as if this story is no surprise.

I glance back at Pete. I'm still uneasy, but his story and the way he tells it seem authentic. Handing his license back to him, he gives me $2.56 in change, still smiling about me seeing his personal information. Maybe he thinks this is an "in" with me.

"Thanks, Leah. See you in a few months for your inspection, right? Unless you want to get coffee sometime."

I give him an uncomfortable smile. "Thank you, Pete. See you in a few months." I don't answer his question about coffee, but he knew I wasn't going to. He asks me out every time I get my car looked at.

Wendy says goodbye to Donna, and we exit the shop. "You know," Wendy says, "Pete is pretty cute. Why don't you take him up on the coffee?"

I bristle, because we just had this conversation four days ago, and it ended with me walking home in the dark. "I'm just not interested, Wendy." I add softly, as an afterthought, "Not yet. Maybe someday."

Wendy looks momentarily shocked that I changed my tune, even slightly. She decides to leave it at that and not push further.

We say our goodbyes and promise to meet up later this week. We're both free Saturday night, so I'm sure Wendy will talk me into doing something out of the house that I don't really feel like doing.

I start heading home, then realize there is nothing in my fridge for dinner. I don't want to go back to Sanderson's for the second time today. I already felt foolish enough being there when I wasn't working, so I drive over to FoodMart.

I'm doing a quick lap around the store, getting staples for the next few days, when I feel a tap on my shoulder.

I jump, shocked that again this week someone has managed to sneak up on me. I've been so good for years about staying alert, and now I've been surprised twice.

Thankfully, it's just Shelly, the woman I made the rash cream for.

"Hi... Leah, right? I didn't get to properly thank you for what you did for me the other day. It worked so well that I didn't even need a prescription. You should really consider bottling that stuff; it's a miracle cure." She sets down her basket and pulls up her sleeves to show me her arms. The skin looks healthy and clear again, no sign of the terrible rash she had the other day.

"Oh, well... I'm glad it worked so effectively. Looks like it's all cleared up." I don't know what else to say. I fidget with the strap on my bag, hoping the conversation is over.

Shelly can see I'm uncomfortable and takes it easy on me. "Yeah, it is." She hands me 20 dollars. "Thanks again!"

Before I can tell her to keep it, she has already walked off to finish her shopping. It would be worse to go after her to give it back, so I put it in my wallet and slip away, somehow even more embarrassed.

I pay for my things, then head out to the car. As I'm putting my groceries in the trunk, I look over and see a white van parked in a parallel spot at the very back of the lot, near the road.

It's unsettling. It's just sitting there, but I keep my eye on it anyway.

As I'm finishing up stowing my purchases for the ride home, I turn and see Mina walking toward me.

She gives me a wave and a small smile. "Hey, Leah, how are you doing? What are you up to?"

I smile at her too, happy to see her again. "I'm doing fine, how are you, Mina? I was just grabbing some groceries. I was on the way home from the auto repair shop and realized I have nothing in my fridge."

She looks concerned. "Oh? What happened to your car?"

I shrug. "Got a flat tire the other day. It happens, not a huge deal. I'm just glad it wasn't a costly repair. Are you here buying more TV dinners?" I giggle slightly.

She blushes. "No, getting some things for my folks. They like to use me as a courier when I'm home. But at least they cook as long as I pick it up. And there are pretty much always leftovers."

The conversation dwindles slightly, as neither of us is sure what to say next. I am happy to have gotten to know Mina a little bit on our walk the other day, and it crosses my mind that she is the first person besides Wendy that I've spoken to in forever that I don't feel an overwhelming need to run away from when we're talking. I have a crazy thought, and before I think it through, it's out of my mouth.

"Hey, did you want to grab a coffee? There's a place near the town center, actually right near Sanderson's, that has a decent menu." As the words leave my lips, I'm thinking, what in hell's name am I doing? Why do I feel disarmed enough around this woman that I just invited her, still very much a stranger, out for coffee? Am I really going to sit across from her and talk? Two things that I haven't done with anyone but Wendy in quite literally years.

Mina seems to contemplate for a second, then replies, "Well, I have to grab the stuff on this list for my parents and then get it home, but I could meet around five, if that works for you. Is it Bean Scene that you're talking about?" She smiles and brushes the hair out of her eyes.

I'm almost as shocked that she accepted as I am that I asked in the first place. "Yeah, that's the one. Five works for me. See you there!"

I get in the car and watch her walk into the grocery store.

What on earth am I doing? I'm torn between feeling comfortable with Mina and feeling like this is another mistake. The mistakes I've made this week have my life feeling like a wheel of Swiss cheese.

I put the car in reverse and back out of the spot, but as I do, I see Carla walking into FoodMart. She sees me, so I give her a polite smile and wave. She gives me a huge grin and waves back.

On the drive home, the setting sun is bright, shining directly in my face. I pull down the visor to block some of it out. As I'm tilting it, a card falls out onto the floor. I don't want to be a distracted driver, so I leave it until I'm securely parked in front of my place.

I bend down, pick it up and study the front. It's blue with decorative flowers and shiny gold woven through the leaves. I don't recognize it, and I know I didn't leave it in my visor.

Maybe it's Pete's, and he put it there, intending to grab it when he was done fixing the car and forgot about it.

I open the card. Handwritten in bold, almost block letters, is the phrase:

THINKING OF YOU

It startles me. I scan the street, as if someone had just placed it into my hands.

Unease consumes me, and I grab my groceries and run inside, locking my deadbolts behind me.

Fifteen

Once I put my purchases away, I take the card off the counter to study it again. It's an innocuous enough greeting card.

It's probably Pete's, that's the only thing that makes any sense, unless I'm missing something.

I decide that I'm done worrying about every little thing, and I'm just going to call and ask. I can confirm Pete left it accidentally, and then I can be on my way to meet Mina for coffee.

Am I really doing that?

I call the number and am greeted with Donna's shrill "Pete's Garage!"

I ask if I can talk to Pete for a minute, but she tells me he's out towing and asks what's wrong. I tell her that I found a greeting card in my car that I assume is Pete's, and he forgot it over my visor.

She promises to have him call me when he's back.

I hang up and set the phone down on the counter. I stare at it a moment, as if maybe it has the answer to this riddle.

When it doesn't provide one, I decide on a quick shower. The warm water comforts me, convinces me that everything is okay. Pete will call back and confirm the note is his, and I can move forward with my life.

Smelling of soap and lavender, I get back in the car to meet Mina for coffee.

My palms are sweating, and I ask myself again what I'm doing. Meeting someone for coffee opens me up to her asking ME questions. I got away with just prying into her life last time; this time, she is undoubtedly going to ask me questions that I can't answer.

I consider turning around and going home, but she's the first human I've connected with in so long that I know I can't do that.

I pull in, and there's a spot right in front of Bean Scene, so I gladly take it. I walk in, and it's still a few minutes before five, so she isn't here yet. I order herbal tea and find a spot against the wall, where I have a good vantage point of the door, and nobody can sneak up on me.

The barista calls out "Lee!" and since I'm the only one here, it must be mine. Maybe she thinks the "H" is silent, who knows.

I'm looking around, taking in the artsy decor and low lighting in the seating area, when Mina walks in.

She spots me immediately and waves, then goes to the counter to order. Her demeanor changes as she places her order. She looks shy, almost timid. She waits at the counter for her coffee to be finished and then comes over to sit across from me.

She seems dejected.

I have been watching people for so long that I have a good sense of how they feel. I can read people's emotions on their faces. "What's wrong?" I ask.

She looks at me for a moment and then turns her coffee cup around so I can read the name the barista wrote on it. "*Willa,*" it says.

"Oh," I say softly. "You went to school with her?"

"Yeah," she sighs.

I get the feeling she wants to open up but doesn't know how or if it's appropriate.

I gently, shockingly, reach out and put my hand over hers. "It's okay," I hear myself saying. "How well do you know her?"

She looks uncomfortable and slowly moves her hand away. I put mine back in my lap, feeling slightly victorious for having made that small gesture.

"We went to high school together," she starts. "She was one of the popular girls who made my life hell. When I came in, I was hoping she wouldn't recognize me, but she did."

"I'm sorry, Mina," I try to comfort her. "She doesn't have power over you anymore. Things have changed a lot since high school."

"They have, and my life outside Ashbourne is so different from what I ever could have imagined as a teenager, but whenever I'm here, I'd rather be anywhere else."

She's tense now, having this woman who was once her tormentor working not fifteen feet away.

I grab her coffee cup and peel off the yellow sticker. Then I take a Sharpie from my purse and write "MINA" in all caps directly on the side of the cup. I hand the label back to Mina to throw away and slide the cup back towards her, with her name facing her.

She smiles, and I can tell it makes her feel slightly better.

"You know what, why don't we get out of here?" I stand, signaling that I'm serious.

Mina looks startled. "Are you sure? Where do you want to go?"

"I don't know, but I don't want to stay here." I whisper a quick thought to her, and she actually smiles.

Mina stands as well, and we move toward the door. As I open it, Mina turns around and says casually, "Hey, Becky, nice seeing you!"

The barista looks confused and says, "Um, my name is Kendra?"

Mina flashes her a huge smile and retorts, "Oh, right. Totally forgot your name, sorry. Have a great night, Cassandra!"

Kendra's mouth hangs open, and before she can think of what to say, we are out the door and on the sidewalk.

Mina and I are giggling like we've been friends for years.

"Oh my God," Mina says, trying to breathe between laughing fits, "did you see her face?"

"I did, and it was such poetic justice." I'm so glad I helped the interaction with Kendra end on a note that will stick with Mina for a long time.

As the laughing fit turns to continued chuckles, we realize we have to decide whether we want to go somewhere else or call it a night.

There isn't much else open on weekday evenings besides Sanderson's, Root and FoodMart. I don't want to hang out at two of those three places, and I know Mina isn't comfortable at Root.

"Well," Mina says, "what do you want to do? There isn't much open. There's a place we could go hang out in the car, but I don't know how comfortable you are with that or how appealing it sounds."

My breath catches. I inhale deeply and then ask, "What's the place?"

If she were out to hurt me, she easily could have yesterday in the woods. My gut is still telling me that she isn't a threat and is maybe as lonely as I am, at least here in Ashbourne.

She laughs, a little uneasy. "Well, it's technically the make-out spot that everyone frequented when we were teens. But there's a beautiful view of town, and we can have our drinks uninterrupted by Becky," she laughs again at our stunt in the coffee shop.

It's early enough that the sun hasn't set, but it will soon enough. Do I have the confidence in my gut to go on such a personal outing with someone I barely know? I like Mina. A lot, actually, but I'm not sure if it's the right call.

Mina senses my hesitation and adds, "It's okay if you don't want to go. We could also sit in your car here in front of Bean Scene, finish our drinks and then go home."

That feels like the adult version of your parents telling you to "leave the door open" to your room as a teen when your boyfriend is over.

I replay what I know about Mina in my head. She grew up here. She knows Wendy and many other locals. She's had two solid opportunities now to hurt me if that was her goal, and she hasn't. I decide that I'm going to trust her, which is a massive step for me. "No, that's kind of silly. Let's go. Just don't put the moves on me."

She laughs, and we walk toward her car.

Sixteen

During the drive up to "The Point," as Mina calls it, we fall into an easy silence.

About ten minutes later, we pull into a clearing. There's a great view of Ashbourne and the sunset. We sit in the idling car, enjoying our drinks and the view.

"So," I say. "How much longer are you visiting until you go back to Boston?"

Mina fidgets with her coffee. "Well, initially I was supposed to go back on Saturday, but my mom hurt her back yesterday, and the doctor said she needs to rest up. I just extended my stay by at least a week." She looks weary, like she really doesn't want to stay here. "Thankfully, I don't have to travel for a while, so it will give Mom time to get back on her feet."

"Are you taking any time for yourself while you're here? You can't just work and wait on your parents."

She smiles wryly. "Isn't that what I'm doing right now?"

I roll my eyes. "I mean, I guess? But grabbing a coffee once in two weeks isn't really self-care."

She looks out at the town, now lit up like Christmas in the darkness below. "It's honestly fine. I don't really live my life here anymore. I have hobbies and my sanity back at home."

I realize that we're alike, but on opposite ends of the spectrum. Neither of us really wants to be here. My past has grounded me in Ashbourne without much say; this IS her past, and she hates the constant reminder.

We're both running from it.

We finish our drinks, and the rest of our conversation is casual: the weather for this week, me choosing herbal tea because of the time of night, and more laughter about "Becky."

It's surprisingly easy to talk to Mina, as if she somehow knows that I don't want to talk about my past. She doesn't dig, and she doesn't ask questions that make me uncomfortable. It's like she understands me on a level that even Wendy doesn't.

I check my phone and realize it's now 8 p.m. I have no idea where the last three hours went, but I'm tired.

Mina says she is too, and we back out of our spot at The Point, driving past two or three cars that undoubtedly contain teenagers, judging by the steamed-up windows.

Mina pulls up behind my car, still parked in front of Bean Scene.

Kendra is just leaving. She must have closed up tonight.

Mina rolls her window down and waves, "Bye, Cassandra! Have a great night!" She rolls the window back up, and we collapse into another round of laughter as Kendra looks at us, disgusted, and walks over to a car that's waiting for her.

"You know," I say, as my own laughter starts to subside, "you could do something like this with every townie who still lives here. It may give you some actual closure. Honestly, why do you care what Kendra, or any of them, thinks of you at this point? I mean, she works at Bean Scene—what a life she's made for herself."

I flinch, realizing I'm talking about Kendra this way, when my own life isn't much better. "Sorry," I add sheepishly. "I have no right to talk."

Mina looks at me sternly and says, "Don't you ever put yourself on the same level as someone like Kendra. I'm surprised she even spelled 'Willa' correctly. You are smart, funny and kind. Don't let anyone make you feel small and especially don't take it from yourself."

I give her a grateful smile and a genuine "Thank you." I had a fun night tonight. I don't do many unpredictable things these days, and tonight was highly unexpected. I'm glad I trusted my gut.

This time, I say, "Let's hang out again sometime."

She smiles and agrees it's a good idea.

I wave goodbye as I get into my car, and Mina drives away.

I had such a good time tonight. I felt normal for the first time in forever. I check my phone, and it's 8:30 p.m.

I realize I have a voicemail. I must not have had service up at The Point. I'll check it when I get home.

Stepping into the house, I shut the door behind me and lean on it heavily.

For the first time (okay, the second), I've trusted a stranger and nothing went wrong. It was actually a fun night, and I'm more relaxed than I ever could have imagined.

I take Maisie out and do my bedtime routine before crawling into bed.

As I lie staring at the ceiling, I realize I'm happy.

It catches me off guard.

I spend my life on high alert. My nervous system is always working overtime, compensating for my overworked brain.

Is it possible? Do I have the ability to be happy here in Ashbourne?

I clutch the blankets to my chin as I let the thought settle.

Maybe I have the capacity to create a real life here.

Only time will tell.

I sleep pretty well, again. It's a nice habit to be forming, and it definitely affects my moods.

Picking up my phone, I realize I never checked the voicemail from last night.

I punch in my PIN, and it's a message from Pete.

"Hi, Leah. It's Pete. Donna told me you found some kind of note or greeting card in your car that you thought might be mine. It isn't, so feel free to throw it away. Thanks, and have a good day."

I feel the hairs on my neck rise, and a chill runs down my spine, thinking about the card.

THINKING OF YOU

For a few hours, I had actually relaxed and nearly let all my worries slip away. The fear and uncertainty are back in full force. I've been less careful this week, and now I'm feeling the echo of that in this greeting card.

It's still entirely possible that someone put it in my car by mistake, or Pete picked it up off the ground and assumed it was mine. It could have been such a small act that it slipped his mind completely, and he doesn't remember doing it. The one thing I'm sure of is that I didn't put it above my visor.

I sit on the floor next to Maisie as she's eating her breakfast. Petting her calms me and keeps me sane when I know I'm spiraling. I tell myself that I've been here two years and nothing that I've been afraid of so far has turned into anything.

Hard as I try, I can't stop waiting for things to go sideways.

I sigh and put my head in my hands. Why did my life turn out like this? I am so tired of being terrified over such small things. Things that are nothing.

I make a choice.

Getting up, I grab the card off the counter and walk over to the kitchen sink.

I take a lighter from my junk drawer and watch as the card slowly blisters in the flames.

When it gets too close to my fingers, I drop it and watch as the remainder of it disappears to ash.

Not having the physical card will make it less likely that I will keep dwelling on it.

I brush the ash from my hands and rinse it all down the sink.

Something still feels wrong, but I cling to the idea that the card was a fluke.

I stroke Maisie's back, even though she's now in her dog bed, snoring away and oblivious to my attention. Despite the last few days of bad luck and strange coincidences, I feel settled in a way I haven't in a long time. I should still be spiraling from the card, but burning it brought me calm I didn't expect.

I think I'm comfortable. Maybe my life can shift, just a little, without exposing me to the larger world.

Seventeen

I have work at 8 a.m. today, so I rush through my morning routine. A quick round of Pilates, breakfast, headlines, a quick shower and then I'm out the door on my way to work.

I'm in at 7:45, which gives me time to make sure everything is clean and the closing tasks from the prior night were done properly.

Bill pops his head out, "Good morning, Leah! How are you today?"

"So far, so good, Bill. No complaints." I'm busy wiping down the counter that was left unwashed last night.

"Okay, sounds good. Brianna should be here any minute to help you open." He slips back out to his painting room.

It's Friday, but I know Brianna will not only be late; she'll also likely be hungover. She's nice and keeps to herself, but she's young and is a party girl, despite being extremely shy at work.

I open up right at eight and have already served seven customers before Brianna slinks in at 8:15. "Hey, Leah," she says quietly. "Sorry I'm late, I had a hard time getting up this morning."

"No worries, Brianna. It hasn't been too busy yet." I try to be kind. She seems fragile, as if she might fracture if you put pressure on her.

She slips out back, cheeks pink, grateful to disappear again. She likes to avoid the register and will gladly stock and clean all day to avoid customers so that I can sit at the counter and cash people out.

It's an easy shift. Most people aren't here to chat with me, and I've gotten used to the face time with so many people all day long. It's automatic now, and half the time I don't even look up.

Brianna is on break, and I'm stocking shelves when I hear the door open.

I look up, and it's Carla.

Great.

A moment later, I realize she isn't here to bother me. She appears to be leading an elderly woman around the store, helping her find the items she needs.

She briefly comes over to me, but only to ask if we have more white rice.

I tell her we don't but point her toward the brown rice.

She thanks me with a smile and continues helping the old woman with her shopping.

Carla really isn't so bad. She's a good person who seems just to be playing the cards she was dealt. She's never done anything to me other than annoy me, but I know that's also a "me" problem.

I'm uncomfortable with attention from anyone, and Carla is a busybody.

Who knows? In another life, we may have been friends if I weren't so irreversibly broken.

I'm stocking the shelf near the beer case and notice a pair of children's safety scissors on the floor.

Weird.

I pick them up, turn them over once, and walk them back to the counter, setting them on a shelf under the register. Maybe they'll come in handy later.

It's the last hour of my shift, and I'm biding my time. The store is empty. Brianna quietly approaches the counter and lurks near the stools, as if she's waiting for me to notice her.

"What's up, Brianna? Do you need something?" I ask.

She looks at me shyly and starts a sentence but stops again. I can't imagine being this painfully embarrassed to exist.

She tries again. Clearing her throat, she says quietly, "I heard that you've been making holistic remedies for people."

I shift uncomfortably in my chair. I'm still not used to being talked about in town, and the idea of becoming "the holistic remedy woman" gives me a tightness in my chest that I can't shake.

Brianna notices my discomfort and withdraws. "I'm sorry, Leah. I won't mention it again." Her shoulders slump and she starts to walk away slowly.

"Brianna," I hear myself saying. "Is there something you need?"

Why am I engaging? She was going to leave me alone.

She turns, and we make eye contact for possibly the first time, despite her being at Sanderson's for the last year.

Her eyes fill with tears, and I'm shocked into silence. I want to help comfort her, but I don't know what's wrong or even how to start.

Brianna looks at the floor as tears roll down her face. "We lost my dad last year. Cancer. It was really quick, and we didn't have much time to get used to it before we had to say goodbye. I've had trouble sleeping ever since. I end up drinking, hoping that it will help me sleep, but it really doesn't. I'm exhausted all the time." Her quiet crying turns into shuddering sobs, and Bill pokes his head out from the back.

"What on earth is going on out here? Leah, did you pinch her or something? What happened?" Bill is beside himself, not knowing what to do with the sobbing young store clerk.

"I've got this, Bill. Can you watch the register for a few minutes?"

Bill agrees, and I take her out back to the break room to help calm her down.

I get her a glass of water. "First, I'm so sorry, Brianna. I had no idea. Of course I can help. I know many herbs that can help calm you down and prepare you for sleep, but you may also need some meditation strategies. I can text you some audio files; all you need to do is sit and listen for about 30 minutes before bed." My chest tightens, thinking about what she's been going through.

She sobs harder, then gets up and gives me a big hug.

I startle, but I accept the hug and put my arms around her too, letting her cry into my shoulder.

"Thank you, Leah," she sobs. "I didn't have anyone I could ask for help."

"It's going to be okay, I promise," I hear myself saying. "If my herbal remedies don't work, Wendy will be able to prescribe something that will. There are lots of options, and we'll find the right one to get you through this."

Standing in the break room, hugging Brianna, is not how I saw my day unfolding when I woke up this morning, but here we are.

Her sobs turn into sniffles. She takes some deep breaths, sips her water and starts to calm down. "Thank you," she says again.

I tell her to take 10 minutes to relax and pull herself together. I can hold down the store until she's ready to come back out front.

I re-emerge from the break room, and Bill looks at me curiously, but I shake my head at him.

He seems to understand there is nothing more he can do, so he goes back to his painting room.

A few minutes later, Brianna returns, and her eyes are red, but she gives me a small smile and goes back to stocking shelves.

My guilt swells. I shouldn't have judged her. She's young and has had a hard year. I assumed her drinking was because she was a party girl, when in reality, she's just trying to survive. I have some things to pick up and some audio to send her, but I'm certain that between Wendy and me, we can help her.

By this point, my workday is essentially over. I pop in the back to say goodbye to Bill and give Brad a wave on my way out.

Brianna leaves at the same time, so walking out, I get her number and tell her I'll be in touch at some point tomorrow.

I slump against my car.

How did I get here? I've been trying for years just to exist, unnoticed, and now I'm drawing needless attention. Granted, it's for a good reason, I'm helping people, but it increases my anxiety.

And that's one thing I have no shortage of.

Instead of going straight home, I make a quick stop at Root.

Wendy is busy today, but I'm not here to see her. I'm picking up a few things that will help Brianna. I grab a small vial of "anti-anxiety oils" for myself at the same time. I dab it on my wrist and neck, even giving Wendy a quick hug before heading home.

I take a deep breath and let the calming scent soothe my nerves.

The sky is pink and gold with the early setting sun, and it's a beautiful view.

Pulling up to my apartment building, I think about how my life is changing. What might it mean for me?

I wonder if Mina is having similar thoughts about our hangout last night.

I consider what else I may need to help Brianna.

By the time I get out and start to walk up to my place, I feel calmer. I'm not sure if it's the oils, the blooming friendship or knowing that what I'm doing for Brianna actually matters, but I'm content.

Maybe there is hope for me after all. I take a deep breath as I contemplate the possibility of a more normal life.

As I approach the steps to my porch, I hear kids playing in the yard next door. Their shrieks of laughter echo through the still evening.

Smiling, I take the stairs to my door.

As I start to pull back the storm door, I feel a blast of heat and notice that my front door is partially open.

I step back in shock, my heart rate spiking, breathing ragged.

Someone is in my house.

Eighteen

The police clear my place in less than a minute. Not much of a footprint to cover. They check my room, the shower, and my closets and find nothing.

All of the windows are still locked, and there is no evidence of any tampering.

I enter timidly, and Maisie is ecstatic to see our uniformed guests and me.

Nothing appears to be missing or destroyed, but I keep looking because if someone broke in, they had a motive.

As unreasonable as it is, I find myself checking the fridge and the silverware drawer.

I know nobody is here, but the whole situation feels wrong in a way I can't fix.

The officers move to leave, making the comment, "Sometimes people forget to lock their doors," but I never forget to lock my door.

I try to press the point, but they are polite and uninterested. Without anything missing or destroyed, there is no crime to report.

As they're departing, they tell me that if anything turns up missing, I can give them another call.

Every nerve in my body is firing now. I don't feel safe in my own home, the one place that I used to be able to relax.

The lack of evidence that someone was here makes it somehow worse. I could rationalize a burglary, though I don't have much worth stealing.

Maybe that's what happened? Someone took the time to break in, took a look around my sparse living space, then turned around and left?

The police questioned my neighbors, but nobody had heard or seen anything unusual.

I did misplace my keys briefly the other day. Could that be something?

No, that's ridiculous.

This means one of two things: either someone was sending me a message, or I truly did forget to lock the door.

Given the lack of evidence, option one seems unlikely. If someone was trying to scare me, why not take something, or worse, leave something? But me, as hypervigilant as I am, forgetting to lock or even CLOSE the door, seems impossible.

I call Wendy to see what she's doing tonight. It's an enormous ask, but I want to know if she'll stay over. I can't be here alone; every creak makes me want to jump out of my skin.

When I tell her what happened, she says she'll get someone else to close Root for her, and she'll be over ASAP.

I sit out on the porch with Maisie pressed against me. I can feel the weight of the world on my shoulders. The warmth of her small body is little comfort right now.

Despite the sun setting beautifully to the west of us, the crimson and gold rays are followed by nothing but darkness. There's no joy. It feels hollow, like the buzzing glow of a fluorescent bar sign.

I wonder if I'll ever feel safe again. I draw in a breath and try to exhale slowly, but I'm shaking, my body trembling with chill and stress.

Twenty minutes later, Wendy announces herself with a text and then a phone call before knocking on the door, so as not to further scare me.

She brings in a pizza and wine, and we decide to eat sitting on the floor. It's one of those actions that is weirdly calming for no reason other than it's a reminder of being young.

Having Wendy here is a salve for me. Being able to sit and eat while recounting my night, telling her my worst fears (or what I'm able to of them), and just generally trying to blow off the steam left over from my scare is helpful in ways she can't imagine.

There's a lull in the conversation while we're both chewing. I zone out, running through all the possibilities again.

"Can I tell you what I think?" Wendy asks gently.

I look up from the floor, already knowing what she's about to say.

"Look around." She gestures to my apartment. "Even if somebody was here, they didn't take anything, and they didn't stick around waiting for you. Maybe they had just gotten the door open, and Maisie spooked them by barking, so they ran." She scoots over beside me, and I put my head on her shoulder. "The point is, what happened was scary, there's no doubt about it. But don't make it more than it is. Whoever was here wasn't out to get you."

I know she's right, deep down. I know I'm overly anxious about literally everything, so of course I'm spiraling now. This is why I needed her here, to ground me back in reality. "Thank you," I say to her in a voice just above a whisper.

She puts an arm around me in a half-hug, and I let my tears fall. Big, silent tears streak down my face and leave small rivulets behind.

She pats my hand and lets me cry, without another word.

For a while, we sit quietly in the moment, and I allow myself to be comforted.

Finally, I lift my head again and face Wendy. I can't believe I'm about to do this, but somebody needs to understand why I'm the way I am. Why I don't trust people, why I hide away from existence. Wendy is the only person in the world I trust enough with my story.

"Three years ago," I begin, "I was out for a run."

Wendy's eyes go wide as she realizes I'm going to, again, trust her with some of my past. Of what shaped me into who I am today. She nods because she doesn't want to interject with her own voice.

"I used to run nearly every day; it was one of my favorite hobbies. Well, on this particular day, I was running in a beautiful but secluded park about two miles from home. I loved that park, partially because it was always inexplicably empty. I was listening to music and trying to maintain my breath and pace when suddenly two men were in my path. My first thought was a mugging, but it was so much worse. They grabbed me, and I kicked and screamed as they threw me in the back of a van."

Wendy gasps; she can't even fathom what I'm currently telling her. She grabs my hand, holding it tight, as I continue.

"I was screaming like my life depended on it, because I was sure it did. I had a chloroform rag stuffed in my face, and I passed out. When I came to, I was in a hospital bed, and I freaked out: just screaming, and screaming. Completely inconsolable." I pause and look up at Wendy.

Tears have formed in her eyes. I can tell that she feels sympathy for what I went through, but also guilt for all the times she's rolled her eyes at me for being so paranoid. "Leah, I..." she trails off.

"It's okay," I tell her. "How could you have known? I don't tell anybody what happened to me."

"Did you ever find out who did it?" She asks.

I continue. "Well, after I woke up in the hospital, it took two nurses and a sedative to calm me down."

I take a deep breath to steady my nerves before I continue. "Once I realized I wasn't still in danger, I was able to calm down enough to talk to the police. I was extremely lucky that the deserted park had one other person in it that day. They saw what happened, immediately called the police, and were smart enough to get the license plate number. The van never even made it to its intended destination. I have no idea where they had planned to bring me."

Wendy is crying now, her chest wracked with sobs that she can't control.

This time, I'm the one who leans in and hugs her. She buries her head in my chest and continues crying. We sit there for a few minutes until she calms down.

"What happened to the guys who grabbed you? Did they go to jail? Did they ever admit to what they were trying to do?"

I'm weary now, emotionally spent. I'm not sure how much I have left tonight. Revealing my past to Wendy is the most vulnerable thing I've done in three years. "Yes, and no. They did go to jail, but the police couldn't get a confession out of them. They were let out on bail, and they disappeared."

Wendy sits upright. "What do you mean, disappeared?"

"I mean just that. They disappeared without a trace. The police have no idea what happened to them." I take a deep breath. I'm so glad that this is out in the open and that Wendy knows now.

"Oh my God," she says, almost angrily. "No wonder you're constantly looking over your shoulder! This is why you live your life as if someone is out to get you, because the worst-case scenario has already happened to you!" She starts crying again, understanding dawning in the most horrifying way.

"It's okay, Wendy," I say, drawing her into my lap and stroking her hair. "I've lived with this for years now. Yes, it's what led me to be as nervous and vigilant as I am about my safety, but that doesn't make you any less right about what happened today. If someone were out to get me, they would have been hiding in a closet, not leaving the front door open. I wouldn't have had the opportunity to call the police first."

She looks up at me, her eyes red and watery. "You are an absolute warrior, you know. To have survived what you did and come out the other side a functioning human."

I snort. "I don't know about 'warrior' or 'functioning' being appropriate ways to describe me," I say with a short laugh. "I was really, really lucky that day, that's it."

We are both quiet for a while. I realize it's getting late. "So, I know we've never had a sleepover here before. Did you want to share my bed with me or sleep on the couch? It's only a full mattress."

"Um, I am not leaving your side until morning. So I'm not staying on the couch unless you are." She looks defiant now.

I put my hands up. "Okay! That's fine, I was just gauging your comfort level. The bed it is, just like high school kids."

We crawl into the bed, and Wendy takes the side near the window. Maisie is unhappily sleeping at the foot of the bed tonight, though once she's asleep, you'd never have known she had a complaint. Wendy is also asleep in minutes, the emotional toll from tonight pulling her right under.

I lie in the dark, listening to Maisie's snoring and Wendy's quiet breathing; to the wind outside, and the owl hunting. I'm searching for my true feelings about today, about my abduction, about my life right now. I decide that overall, I feel better.

I get up one last time to check the locks on the door and the windows.

They're secure.

I crawl back under the covers and fall into an uneasy sleep.

Nineteen

I wake the next morning, and Wendy is in my kitchen making bacon and eggs. A fresh pot of coffee is waiting for me.

Maisie waits hopefully for bacon.

Over breakfast, I tell Wendy about Brianna's issues.

She listens intently while chewing on toast. "Well, I think something homeopathic is the best starting point. It may or may not help, but like you told her, we will keep trying until something does. We should also give her the number of that therapist in Wayfield. She needs to talk to someone and process what she's been through."

Wendy is a huge proponent of therapy. I don't personally *disagree* with the idea of therapy. It just didn't really help me for multiple reasons.

She puts down her toast and brushes the crumbs off her lap. "Can we talk about yesterday? I don't want to harp on everything you told me. I just want you to know how honored I am that you opened up to me. If you ever want to talk about it, if talking through it will help you work through it, I'm here."

I smile. "Thank you for listening and understanding. I know it creates a whole different picture of why I am the way I am. I'm relieved that you have a bit more understanding now."

Wendy's smile falters. "Are you going to be okay today? I'm supposed to work this morning, but if you need me, I can either call someone else in or just close for the day. I don't want to leave you alone if you aren't comfortable."

I hesitate, thinking of how I felt when I got home yesterday and found my door ajar. But I also realize that everything Wendy has said makes sense. If someone were out to hurt me, they would have hidden in my apartment with the door shut and locked.

This thought sends a shiver down my spine, but that isn't what happened. The most likely thing is that someone tried to break in, Maisie scared them off, and they high-tailed it out of there without bothering to shut the door. "I'll be okay," I tell her.

She looks at me and cocks her head to the side as if to say, *really?*

I nod. "I'll be fine. Everything you said last night makes too much sense to ignore."

She sighs, picking up her fork. "Okay." She points the fork at me. "But you'd better call me if you're not okay. Even if it's three hours from now." She goes back to eating her scrambled eggs.

We finish breakfast, and Wendy leaves for home to shower before work. I'm off today, so I lie on the couch reading headlines. I'm too full for yoga.

There's an interesting article about a new drug that could revolutionize fighting cancer, which is exciting. I continue scrolling down the page until I see another article that makes my stomach drop.

ChemGen to Resume Production Next Year

ChemGen (C-GEN), an industrial medicine powerhouse that lost its pharmaceutical licensing rights three years ago due to negligence claims, has been bought by NeroGen (No-Ge) and is poised to reopen its closed branch by mid-next year. They previously specialized in gene therapy and gene editing advancements.

I turn off my tablet and know that I need to get out of here and clear my head. I grab Maisie's leash and take her outside, double-checking that I locked the door behind us. We turn left and walk toward the town center. I know I can't take Maisie into any stores, but I don't want to be anywhere remote right now.

I think about our last walk around the lake and wish that I had more courage. It would be nice to head back out that way; it's so beautiful, and the air feels cleaner out there.

We stick to the streets in town and do several laps past Sanderson's and Root. I wave at Wendy each time we walk past, and she laughs and rolls her eyes at me.

On my fourth lap around, I run into Carla.

"Oh, my dear, I heard about what happened last night. A robbery! How terrible. Did they take much?" She looks at me attentively. News travels fast in a small town.

I shift uncomfortably, trying to avoid eye contact. "Well, it wasn't actually a robbery. They didn't take anything."

Carla looks shocked. "Oh my! How do you even know someone was there?" She takes a step closer like she's afraid she might miss my reply.

"The door was open when I got home. I called the police, but they said I must have forgotten to close it on my way out." I bristle at the memory.

Carla can see my agitation, and she reaches out to touch my arm as she tries to console me. "I'm sorry, Leah, that must have been scary and frustrating."

I pull back, recoiling, and she grasps only air.

The look on her face changes for a moment, but she recovers quickly. "Sorry, dear. I forget that you don't like to be touched."

I decide to move the conversation to another subject. "How is Lilly's violin going?"

Carla looks stunned for a moment.

I've never tried to interact with her on a personal level before. She brightens and starts chatting about her little girl being a prodigy and how smart she is. "She's overcome so much, and I couldn't be happier."

"That's wonderful, Carla. I'm so glad Lilly has found something that makes her happy." I wrap up the conversation and say goodbye, because Maisie is dancing around, wanting to continue walking.

The walk home is calming, and it feels nice to just breathe and exist for a moment.

I'm proud of myself lately. Not that my anxiety has lessened or my troubles are over, but that I've taken the initiative to begin truly trusting Wendy. That I've chosen to bridge gaps and reach out, like with Mina. I feel more human now than I have in years, despite all the issues I know haven't gone away.

Maisie and I get home, and everything is as I left it. I double-check the windows and the closets, but deep down, I know things are okay. I can sense it.

I get to work on Brianna's insomnia remedy.

This morning, I texted her to come into Sanderson's tonight to pick it up. She was ecstatic and said she'll be in around six.

Grabbing my kitchen tools, I measure each ingredient to the milliliter.

I should probably get some tools specifically for this kind of thing if I'm going to keep doing it. Eventually, there could be things that shouldn't cross-contaminate with food.

I make a mental note to stop by and get some tools to help this process along, either later today or tomorrow.

Creating these solutions to people's problems causes me social anxiety, but it is also rewarding. Standing at my counter, mixing, knowing that what I'm doing is going to help Brianna, is satisfying in a way I haven't felt in years. It's a feeling I don't get from working at Sanderson's.

I think what I'm feeling is pride.

Twenty

Brianna shows up at six as promised. She looks like she's full of hope, and I'm so glad to be able to help her.

I give her instructions on use and tell her to text me and let me know how it goes. I also send her the meditation files I promised.

When Brianna leaves, she's practically skipping. I get the feeling that even though it's Saturday, she won't be out hanging with friends and drinking tonight. I'm glad I was able to give her back some hope.

It's a typical weekend night in Ashbourne. Families drifting in and out to grab something quick to make for dinner before funneling their kids off to dance or hockey practice. Regulars sit in the social area, playing checkers or arguing about the local sports teams or politics. The store hums with energy as only the weekend can.

A group of older teenagers enters and loiters for a few minutes around the beer case. It seems to be one of the favorite pastimes of Ashbourne's teens, standing at that beer case and wondering if someone will sell to them. Eventually, they decide that they don't have the courage, or that I will card them, and they change course to the snack section.

A moment later, the group sidles up to the register, each with a fistful of chips and candy bars. I cash out the first one, and the others hang back, whispering to themselves. I look up, and they keep glancing at me, then back to their group.

I flush.

I don't care what they're saying, but I don't want the attention. The next child steps up, and I cash them out, then the next.

As I'm finishing bagging the snacks of the last teen, one of the guys in the back of the group says, "Hey, aren't you the woman on Rowan who broke into her own apartment for attention?"

The hair on my neck stands up, and I look at him, shocked. "W-what?" I ask.

He grows bolder and steps forward. "Yeah, I heard that you called the police out because you forgot to shut your own door." His laughter is mean, almost a snarl.

I'm scared. *"The woman on Rowan."* People aren't just talking about me; this isn't only about attention.

They know where I live.

I recoil from the teenager, trying to process what I just learned.

Gripping the counter behind me, I hit full-on panic mode.

I'm sure I look terrified because he stares at me, confused, wondering why taunting me made me scared rather than angry or embarrassed. He was hoping for a reaction that he didn't receive.

He shrugs and heads for the door with the rest of his group, bag of snacks clutched in his hand.

As the door shuts behind them, I can still hear their raucous laughter out in the parking lot. They really thought tormenting me was funny.

Is this rumor only going around the local high schoolers? Or is this circulating all over town?

Does everyone know where I live? I feel more exposed than ever.

I step away from the register, head spinning. I feel sick and need to sit down.

Brad looks up from stocking shelves and sees that I'm not well. He rushes over to the counter. "Are you okay, Leah? What's wrong?"

"I... I just need a minute. Can you please take over the register, Brad?"

I rush out back, then realize I'm going to vomit.

I make it to the employee bathroom just in time.

After, I sit on the closed toilet, sweaty and shaking.

How did this happen? Besides Wendy, who even knows where I live?

Did someone at the police station tell someone else, and was it just a spiderweb of information to the rest of the town from there?

My brows draw together. I didn't call the police "for attention." Attention is absolutely the last thing I want. That detail had escaped me until now, as the panic of people knowing where I live took over.

I hear a knock on the bathroom door. It's Bill.

"You okay in there, Leah? Brad said you didn't look so good." I hear his feet shifting outside the door. He's uncomfortable checking on me, but cares enough that he did anyway.

I open the door and then break down in tears: wracking sobs that consume my entire frame.

Bill looks shaken. He's not used to seeing my emotions; nobody is. "What happened?" He puts his hand on my shoulder.

I instinctively jump, but he doesn't remove his hand. He wants me to know he isn't going anywhere.

"A kid from town asked me about the break-in and insinuated that I did it myself for attention. It's not that part that really bothers me, it's that the whole town must be talking about me, and he specifically mentioned where I live." I continue crying, knowing that it may be a while before it stops. I don't cry often, so when I do, it's like a volcano erupting; the stress I've bottled up will keep coming out until the pressure has subsided.

Bill leads me back to his painting room to sit down. He makes me a cup of tea.

He lets me cry, not pressing me for more information or talking to break the awkward silence. He just stays with me, nothing more.

It's comforting. It's enough.

The tears dry up, but my breath still catches in my chest, and I can't breathe deeply yet.

I thank Bill for the tea and sit, existing. I'm grateful Bill is my friend.

We don't talk about it again. There isn't really much to say. Neither of us has any idea who started the rumor or how they knew where I live. It's a moment of acceptance, soothing in its simplicity.

Bill tells me to go home, that he and Brad can close up tonight.

I thank him and grab my things.

In the car, I wonder if I'll ever feel safe in Ashbourne again. The greeting card, the break-in, this new town gossip that includes the street I live on... How did I become so noticeable?

I've been worried that making holistic remedies for people was putting me too much in the spotlight, and somehow, an action that I had no control over is what has me on everyone's radar.

I get upstairs and, after greeting Maisie, I check the locks on all the windows and peek in the closet.

Once I'm done, I collapse onto the floor, letting Maisie lick my face. I don't have the energy to stop her.

I briefly consider getting takeout, so I don't have to cook, but that requires going back out because I will not give my address to anyone for delivery. Not that it seems to matter that much anymore.

I spend my night rage-cleaning my apartment. I wash windows, vacuum, wipe out all the kitchen cabinets and scrub the toilet until it shines.

When I'm done, the house smells of lemon and window cleaner, and I'm sweaty and exhausted, but I feel slightly better.

The sky outside is leaning into darkness, and I try to let my emotions depart with the last of the light.

I light a candle and leave it on the kitchen counter, then put on an old movie. It's one of my childhood favorites, and it distracts me enough to begin moving on from my feelings right now.

There is nothing I can do about the rumor except let it fizzle out.

I take Maisie out for the last time tonight and wait as she does her business.

The air is cold, but there's no breeze.

Someone nearby is having a bonfire; I can smell the burning wood even though I can't see it. It's quiet, and laughter drifts from the yard across the street where the fire must be burning.

I imagine that the people over there must be huddled together, drinking warm beverages and roasting marshmallows, though that's probably just me projecting my own childhood into the scenario.

We walk back up the stairs, and when I open the door, I notice there's a different smell in the air, like melted wax with the faint scent of burnt wick. I walk over to the counter and see the candle has gone out, a slight curl of smoke still smoldering from the coal-blackened ember. The heat must have kicked on, or the breeze from opening the door might have extinguished the flame.

I don't re-light it; it's time for bed anyway.

Maisie jumps onto the bed, and I check the windows and door for the final time tonight. I curl in next to her and stroke her back as she falls asleep. I'm so glad to have adopted her; she may be the one thing that keeps me sane, living here alone.

I fall asleep trying to process today's events. My dreams are stilted, quick shots of my open door, the teen from Sanderson's today, Carla talking about Lilly. I have no vivid nightmares, but they're not what I would consider "good" dreams either.

I wake before Maisie does, to the sound of her heavy breathing. She's dreaming, and from the looks of it, she's chasing something.

I smile fondly at her, slightly jealous that her dreams are so much simpler than my own.

It's Sunday, and it's warm for November. I'm not working today, so I consider going hiking. I've always loved it, the smell of earth, the heat in my muscles while climbing a steep spot, the view you earn at the top.

I sigh. With my nerves so shot, it might be a pipedream.

Maybe I'll text Wendy?

No, she hates hiking.

Then I have a thought: I don't know Mina well, and I'm not sure we're in the "invite each other hiking" stage yet, but I do really want to go. If I attempt to go alone, I'm going to jump at every breaking of a twig or someone walking by on the trail. I'm skeptical, but before I can talk myself out of it, I send her a text.

Hey, was thinking of hiking today. Want to come?

I put the phone down, my heart beating faster. It's a different kind of fear than I'm used to. I'm usually worried about visibility, not social rejection.

I make a pot of coffee and a light breakfast, in case she replies. I'm finishing up my coffee and yogurt when my phone vibrates.

Sure, where are you going? What time?

My heart skips as I realize I've now put myself in another situation where I'm going to be alone with Mina, far from town. As much as I'm beginning to trust her, there are still lingering doubts. I don't know if I can fully trust anybody but Wendy, or if I ever will again. I text Mina back:

Not sure, any suggestions? Is 9ish good?

She replies quickly.

9 works, how about Stark?

I've never actually hiked around here, so I look up the Stark Mountain trail on my phone. Seems like it's an easier route, lots of winding up the hill to the scenic view.

Sounds good, see you there!

I text her back and then wonder if my exclamation point was too aggressive.

I wrestle with whether to take Maisie with me, then decide that it makes the most sense to leave her home.

If my goal is to de-stress, worrying about picking up after her and carrying a water bowl on a three-hour hike seems like it would do the opposite.

I pack a backpack with a large water bottle and snacks, and then I'm out the door.

Twenty-One

"Thanks for meeting up with me," I tell Mina. "Wendy hates hiking, so I didn't even bother asking."

Mina is dressed in matching workout gear and has actual hiking boots.

I'm in sweats and a light jacket with sneakers, completely mismatched. She must do this fairly regularly, judging by the boots.

"Thanks for inviting me. I love hiking, and being near the city most of the time, it's a hobby I don't get to do regularly." She smiles genuinely as she shifts her hiking pack on her shoulders.

We enter the trailhead and walk side by side as we begin to make our way up the mountain. For a few minutes, we're quiet, taking in the calm of the rocks and trees and the fresh air that smells of pine. Neither of us really knows what we should talk about. I'm reminded again of how briefly I've known her.

Finally, Mina glances at me. "I heard what happened with the break-in. Are you okay?"

I tense. I hadn't thought about how she'd know, but even though Mina doesn't live here anymore, she's still "from here," so of course, she would have heard about it through the grapevine.

"I'm sorry I didn't reach out to check on you," she continues. "I didn't want to pry, and I didn't know how to ask." She looks down, seeming ashamed.

"It's okay," I say. "There was nothing you could have done. Wendy came to stay with me that night. In the end, nothing was taken, and nobody was there, so it seems more like a robbery gone awry. Maybe Maisie chased them off." I keep a steady pace as we climb. It helps, like I'm leaving the fear of the last couple of days behind me.

"Still," Mina says, "It must have been really unsettling. I can't imagine how hard it is to sleep in a house that you know someone may have been in." She senses my unease at this conversation and then pivots.

"So, what kind of music do you normally listen to?"

From there, we make small talk about her growing up here, about me growing up in Northern California. It's still easy to talk about my childhood. I can tell stories all day about the beach, the forests and the mountains.

College never comes up. I assume she thinks I didn't go, which is for the best.

We spend the morning hiking and chatting, stopping a few times for water, once for snacks.

The view from the top is breathtaking; even without leaves, the woods stretch for miles in every direction, dotted by small lakes and ponds that make the landscape feel like a fantasy.

Even though it's chilly, the heat from the hike and the sun sit warmly on my skin.

We begin our descent, which will take less time than the hike up.

Our chatter has been warm and friendly, and I'm glad I asked Mina to join me. It was exactly the morning I had hoped for.

For a moment, we're quiet, taking in the trees and the cool air.

"So, how well do you know Carla?" Mina asks. She's looking at the trail ahead and only glances quickly at me.

"I mean, we certainly aren't *friends*," I say. "She's a nosy customer who loves to hang out at Sanderson's. She's odd, but ultimately, I think she's harmless."

"Yeah, you're probably right," Mina replies. "I get a weird feeling around her, like maybe she has secrets."

We all do, don't we? "Maybe," I say. "I know that she's really protective of Lilly, but I think that's normal."

"True," Mina says. "I can't judge her, I'm sure that she's been through a lot."

Just then, we see a fox scurry across the trail carrying a small rabbit, limp in its mouth. "I guess he found his breakfast," I laugh. I wonder if it's the same fox from the other day, and I'm glad the little guy found a meal.

We exit the trailhead and linger a moment longer, talking about our plans for the weekend. Mina thanks me again for inviting her, and I thank her for coming with me. It was a nice, relaxing morning and exactly what I needed after the last few days.

We say goodbye, then get into our cars to head home, promising to hang out again soon.

The drive is about 30 minutes, and I turn on the radio and hum along to songs from my teen years.

My muscles are tired, and it feels good.

I glance in the rearview mirror and realize I may have gotten a slight sunburn despite the cold. I should have thought to put on sunscreen.

My phone rings. I glance at the seat next to me, but it's an unknown number. It's probably spam.

I don't pick up. It stops ringing, and a moment later the phone buzzes.

1 new voicemail.

I'm not going to check it while driving, I'll wait until I get home.

I pull up in front of the house. Grabbing the phone, I punch in my PIN and click the arrow to listen to the voicemail.

I hear a crackle, like an old recording. I wait for "we've been trying to reach you about your car's extended warranty," but instead, I vaguely hear what sounds like a man delivering a news broadcast, starting mid-sentence.

> *... following the failed ChemGen clinical trial that left multiple people injured, and several in critical condition...*

The voicemail cuts off mid-sentence.

I drop the phone like it just burned me. For a moment, I'm completely frozen. My heart is pounding, and my palms are so sweaty that I can't open the car door. In my head, there's a hum that is more mechanical than natural.

Somebody here knows who I am.

Twenty-Two

I stumble up the stairs in disbelief.

My brain tries to process what just happened. I fumble my keys in the lock, dropping them repeatedly before getting inside. Maybe I heard it wrong? I enter my PIN again and listen.

... following the failed ChemGen clinical trial...

How did this happen? I have spent years being so careful, staying out of the spotlight, avoiding any semblance of a real life.

For a minute, I hope I'm having a break from reality. I listen again. And again.

... following the failed ChemGen...

As I'm sitting on the floor, petting Maisie for comfort, I allow a memory I haven't thought of in years to surface.

I'm at work, staring at a computer screen. The smell of industrial cleaner and isopropyl alcohol permeates the lab. Centrifuges hum in the background. Glass and metal surround me in every direction, as well as piles of printed charts and folders. Each folder contains worse and worse results.

My phone rings and I put my head in my hands before picking up. "Hi, Mom," I answer, sounding completely exhausted.

"Hi, Ellie. How are you, baby? You sound terrible. Have you eaten today? Have you slept?"

I wince. I don't like it when anyone but Nan uses my nickname. "I'm okay, Mom. Just having a terrible week. I made some really poor decisions, and now I'm not sure what to do next."

I take my glasses off and pinch the bridge of my nose, wishing I didn't have to have this conversation with her. She will never understand.

"Oh, honey. I'm so sorry. Do you want to talk about it?" She's making dinner; I can hear the clang of pots and pans in the background.

"No, Mom," I say, too harshly. "It's technical, you wouldn't understand." This isn't the truth, but I can't bring myself to say the truth out loud yet.

"Well," she says, "if you change your mind, you know you can call me anytime. Or if it's really bad, you can always come home. We're here for you with open arms." The pans continue clanging in the background, and I can hear a sizzling sound as she sautés something.

This makes me feel worse, and tears start to escape. "Thanks, Mom. Love you," I say, hanging up.

The tears fall onto the papers, the documentation of all my wrongdoing, spread out like a colorless rainbow around me.

I don't know what I'm going to do.

The lab door opens.

I look up, then sigh and put my head back in my hands. "What do you want?"

"Wow. That happy to see me, huh?" He smiles broadly at me, but I don't smile back.

"I don't want to talk to you right now."

He comes over to my desk and sits on it. "Why, what's up?"

I look at him, shocked. "What's up? Are you kidding? Have you seen these results? This is the biggest nightmare of my career."

He spots a tin of mints on my desk and picks them up. "Oh, I like these." He helps himself to one, then puts the tin down. "What are you so worried about? The results are preliminary." He picks the tin back up and pops two more in his mouth.

My eyes are wide now. "Preliminary? Are you serious?"

Maisie whines, jolting me back to reality. I hug her and cry wracking sobs into her wiry fur. She looks confused, but her tail is still wagging, just happy that I'm paying attention to her.

"Maisie, I really screwed up," I tell her.

She cocks her head to the side, listening intently.

"I have to figure out what we're going to do next. No matter what, you're coming with me."

She licks my face and nudges my hand for more pets.

I take her downstairs to go out. I'm sure she has to pee by now. It's early afternoon and the warmest part of the day.

I sit on the stoop while Maisie frolics in the back yard. She finds a smelly spot to roll in, happy to be outside. I put my head in my hands and try to calm my racing heart with deep breaths, but relief doesn't come.

There's a phone call I should make, but I can't. Can I?

What would I even say? Someone mentioned my old company in a voicemail, and now I'm unraveling?

Even to me, it sounds ridiculous.

Is there a rational explanation?

Companies merge all the time, especially in that industry.

Could it possibly be a coincidence?

Please, let it be a coincidence.

Maisie finishes rubbing herself in the smelly spot and puts her nose to the ground, practically snorting at the dead grass.

I give a sad half-smile. I'm glad she's having a good time.

I'm grateful for the warmth of the sun on my face on this mild day. I don't know what I'm going to do, but I'm going to start with feeding both of us lunch. I call her, and we head back up the stairs to my place.

I'm worn down. My breath has evened out, but I'm sure I look like a wreck. I can smell the panic sweat on myself from my scare. I take the steps slowly, because if I extend our time out here, everything upstairs will stay further away.

We walk inside, and I freeze.

There's a scent in the air that wasn't here earlier. It smells like cinnamon and warm wax.

I step toward the kitchen counter.

The candle is lit.

Twenty-Three

I take a step back, confused. Looking around the apartment, I see it's empty.

I check the locks, the windows, the closets. Nobody is here but Maisie and me.

Did I light this candle?

I don't remember doing that. I have no memory of even going into the kitchen. But everything is locked.

How is this possible?

I think I may be losing my mind. I must have lit the candle. Nobody else is here. All the doors and windows are locked. There is no other explanation.

I sink to the floor in the kitchen, wondering what dregs of sanity I have left.

At least it smells nice, I guess.

I check the voicemail one more time, to be sure it wasn't only a bad dream. Replaying it over and over takes some of the sting out. It feels a little less like a threat each time.

I grab my keys and head back out to town.

Parking in the center, I walk to Root, but Wendy is extremely busy. Plus, what would I even tell her? That I lit a candle and don't remember it? That my old company's name was left in a voicemail to me, and I think it's meant to freak me out?

I go back outside and into the clear but slightly chilled air. It smells like fall, even though it's nearly winter now.

Sitting on a bench, I attempt to clear my head. I close my eyes and try to regulate my breathing, a living meditation in the middle of the hustle and bustle of all the local businesses.

Just as I'm beginning to feel slightly calmer, I hear a voice.

"Hello, dear. You look a little worse for wear today. Everything okay?"

I open my eyes and see Carla staring at me. I don't know what to say to her.

She tilts her head slightly. The unsettling grin appears. "You look pale. Are you not feeling well?"

I start to speak, but my voice catches. I have no idea how to answer her. I thought if I started talking, some reflex would kick in.

It doesn't.

Carla stares at me, and I can't read her.

I think stress has completely broken my senses.

"What's wrong?" she asks.

I sigh. "Carla, I've had a day, and I don't know how to explain it to anyone."

A look of concern crosses her face. "Oh my. Do you want to try to talk about it? I know I'm a talker, but I'm a great listener too, you know."

This is Carla's way of trying to be helpful. She shifts from foot to foot, making it look like she's doing a little dance that seems almost cheerful. I think she's trying to keep her typical barrage of questions to herself.

Her large clothes and pockets seem to sway with her odd, shifting dance.

"No, but thank you, Carla," I say. "I honestly wouldn't know where to start."

We stare at each other for a moment, silent.

Finally, Carla asks, "Did the police get any leads on your break-in?"

I inhale sharply. I didn't need a reminder of yet another thing that has gone wrong over the last few days.

"No," I answer. "They think I left the door open. I know I didn't."

Is it me, or is there a look of superiority on her face?

No, that's not right. She's only watching me closely, as if she can sense my personal unravelling.

Carla's face adjusts, and she looks at me sadly. "Oh, my dear. There's been some talk around town, too. I've heard it myself. I make sure to tell them that you wouldn't have done that, you're very careful."

I hold my head in my hands, and a tear slips out.

Carla backs up slowly, unnerved by my show of emotion, then makes an excuse about having errands to run. She fades into the background, and she's gone.

I sit in the sun, wishing I could be anyone else.

A few minutes pass, and I see Brianna walking towards me. She's just finished her shift at Sanderson's. She looks refreshed, like a weight has been lifted off her shoulders.

"Hi, Leah!" she practically chirps. She doesn't pick up on my current misery.

Hearing her voice grounds me, and I want the normalcy of stocking shelves back. Of sitting, bored, at the register, waiting for my shift to end. "Hi, Brianna, how's it going?"

She gives me a shy smile. "Last night, I had the best night's sleep since my father died. I don't know how to thank you, Leah." She doesn't know what to do with her hands, so she fidgets with a ring she's wearing.

I give her a tired smile. "I'm so glad to hear that. Did you call the number of the therapist I gave you?" I'm glad to have this distraction with Brianna, something else to focus on, worry about, even if it's just for a moment.

"I did. I left her a voicemail. I'm hoping to hear back from her tomorrow. Please thank Wendy for me. I'm so grateful to both of you."

We make small talk for a short while about how busy the store was today and how creepy Brad is, and then she's on her way home.

I continue to sit. Some passersby whisper as they cross my path.

I flinch each time.

Some point from far enough away that they think I don't notice.

But I do.

I'm numb.

Any of these people could have left the voicemail. Each of them may know where I live. The world around me is a distant hum of life continuing on, regardless of my problems.

I look up and see Carla staring at me from outside a store. She probably thinks I'm losing it. She sees me catch her watching, and she turns away.

It's cold again, and I'm starting to lose feeling in my fingertips.

It's time to go home.

At home, the candle is still lit. I forgot to extinguish it when I ran out in a panic.

At least, I think I did.

Maisie is ecstatic that I'm home again, and I lie on the floor and bury my face in her fur. She smells like dog, clean blankets and childhood comfort.

I want to relax, but my day haunts me like a fever dream. I stare into the flame of the fluttering candle, my uncertainty on an endless loop.

Voicemail. Candle. Carla.

Wait, need to feed Maisie.

Voicemail. Candle. Carla.

Do I have anything I can make for dinner?

Voicemail. Candle. Carla.

I go to take a shower, hoping that if I scrub hard enough, I can wash today away. When the water runs cold, my skin is pink from the effort, but it doesn't undo any of it.

Maisie and I go out for the last time tonight. Every little thing has me on edge.

Was that a shadow over there to the left?

No, I imagined it.

What was that noise?

Just the owl.

He's louder than usual.

Why does it smell like cinnamon out here?

The scent of the candle must be stuck in my nose.

Back in the house, Maisie settles onto the bed for the night. I'm changing into pajamas when the phone rings, and I jump.

It's only Wendy.

"Hi, how's it going? I felt bad that I didn't have time to talk when you stopped by earlier, so I thought I'd give you a quick call. You looked pale. Are you alright?" She sounds concerned.

"Hey, yeah, thanks for calling. I had a rough day. Some are worse than others, you know?" I can't tell her about the voicemail, and if I try to explain the candle, she'll just think I'm crazy. "Did you get out of work late?"

"Late? Leah, it's 9:03."

My sense of time is off. My nerves have scrambled everything. "Oh, right. Sorry, didn't realize it was still so early."

"Are you really okay? You sound... off." I can hear the heightened sense of worry in her voice.

I force a smile, hoping it will make me sound lighter. "No, I'm fine. I'll be fine. Thanks for calling."

We hang up, and I put the phone down. It may be just after 9, but I want this day to be over.

I hope that tomorrow I'll wake up and the psychological noose around my neck will feel a little looser.

I tuck myself in. The smell of cinnamon still clings to my hair. I give Maisie a quick hug before turning out the light and falling into a turbulent sleep.

Twenty-Four

I'm running through a forest. The sky is dark as midnight.

Someone is chasing me, but I'm not sure who. I'm not entirely sure that it's even human.

I stop running and hide, concealing myself behind a large tree a few yards to the side. I peek around its trunk, hoping that whatever is tailing me will run right by. I can hear the leaves crunching under its feet.

The figure stops, listening intently.

The moonlight filters through the trees, allowing me to make out its shape.

The figure is dressed in black, with a hood over its head. The robe it's wearing has large pockets all over it. It begins to search through the pockets, looking for something.

It pulls out an orb that is glowing with a ghastly red light. The monster lets go, and the orb hovers, not two feet in front of it. It resumes searching its pockets, pulling out lavender, an inhaler and what looks like file folders.

I shift in my spot behind the tree, accidentally rustling some leaves at my feet. I go stock-still, knowing that if the monster sees me, I'm going to die. My heart beats rapidly, and there is a metallic taste in my mouth. Squeezing my eyes shut, I pray to every deity in existence that it didn't hear me.

The figure stops what it's doing for a moment and listens.

My breath catches in my chest.

It returns to its task, taking all the items and placing them so they hover around the orb, rotating in position. It chants a phrase in a language I don't understand. The items are absorbed into the orb, and it glows brighter and brighter until, in a flash of what seems like daylight, everything is gone. In its hand is a candle. The figure lights it, still chanting.

To my horror, my legs move without my consent. I walk slowly, as if mesmerized, toward the leaf-strewn path where the figure stands. I have no control over my body, and only my face shows the terror I feel inside.

It begins to turn, and with the hood shading its eyes in the moonlight, I can only see its sickening smile.

I realize the orb is still there, hovering at its side. I see my life in quick flashes inside the orb: My 8th birthday party, swim team in high school, the lab. I see a flash of Wendy smiling. Bill painting. Carla. Mina. Then the orb darkens with smoke.

I can smell cinnamon.

I'm now standing directly in front of the figure, and it moves to lift the hood from its face.

The beast is somehow unfamiliar, but also everyone who's ever mattered in my life. The face changes, flicking through facial patterns, until it lands on one.

I scream, an earth-shattering sound that scares me even as it comes from deep inside. Moths fly out of my mouth, and I continue screaming.

The monster with Wendy's face grins at me. It grabs me by the wrist with its icy, skeletal fingers.

It speaks. It's not Wendy's voice, but Carla's.

"What's wrong, dear? You don't like having to pay for your sins?"

The Wendy/Carla monster laughs, an evil sound that chills me to the bone.

I'm shaking. Every fiber of my body tells me to run, but my legs don't work.

As my tears start to fall, the monster goes back to searching its pockets. It returns a syringe and a small glass vial. It fills the syringe and flicks it a few times. Then it turns to me with its sickening smile and plunges it directly into my heart.

"I thought you could use a taste of your own medicine."

Twenty-Five

I bolt awake, head pounding. Daylight pours through my window. It adds confusion to the aftermath of my nightmare.

What time is it?

It's almost eight. I'm going to be late for work.

I call Bill's phone and leave him a voicemail letting him know I'll be 30 minutes late. After a quick shower to rinse off the sweat from my fading nightmare, I gulp down a cup of coffee and an apple.

On the drive to work, I replay the now receding nightmare.

Have I made a mistake? Was trusting Wendy as much as I have wrong?

Is Carla actually a threat?

The only thing I'm certain of is that I'm certain of nothing.

I walk into Sanderson's, and Brad gives me a disapproving glance, but he's busy at the register, so I quickly place my things out back and get to work.

The normalcy of stocking shelves and cleaning is soothing, and it calms me slightly. I keep myself busy for the first few hours, trying to quell my own intrusive thoughts. It helps minimally.

I take my lunch break, and Bill pops out back to check on me.

"You okay, kid? You seem off today." His voice is full of concern.

I smile at him with all the warmth I can muster. "I'm okay, Bill. Just overslept, that's all."

I hope he can't see that my hands are shaking slightly.

He sits with me, not really knowing what else to say. I know he suspects that something more is off; I can sense it. But he doesn't know how to handle it, so he sits while I eat my sandwich.

His presence does somewhat lighten the load. Knowing that he cares if I'm okay counts for something. Doesn't it?

After lunch, I take the register so Brad can break. Mondays are usually steady, with customers hurrying in and out, trying to get their errands done after work.

There's a short lull, and the store is quiet for a moment. A man comes in and looks around. Seeing the store empty, he comes directly to the counter, though he stands back further than is typical. He seems timid and slightly embarrassed.

"Can I help you?" I ask, figuring he wants to know where the condoms are. I see this kind of awkward reluctance pretty frequently.

"Are... are you Leah?" he asks, even though he can see from my nametag that I am.

With my senses so dulled, all I can muster is a minor flinch. "Yes. Can I help you?"

"Um... hi. I was hoping you could help me with a problem I'm having. It's kind of embarrassing." He looks to the floor, then glances back up to see if I'm going to respond.

I don't. I wait for him to continue, my mind spinning with what he might need.

"I... I heard that you make things for people. Like things that help them." He glances at the floor again as he fidgets with his keys.

I exhale. I didn't realize I was holding my breath. This is doable, at this point, a welcome distraction from my current problems. "Oh. Yeah, maybe. Depending on what it is, I may be able to help. What's going on?"

He blushes and starts to explain, but the door opens, and Carla comes in.

She sees I'm helping a customer, so she sits down at the far end of the counter.

"So," he whispers.

I have to lean in to hear him. He's obviously very embarrassed and doesn't want Carla to hear.

"I have a problem with... my breath. I've tried everything: gum, mints, mouthwash. I brush and floss twice a day. Nothing works, and..." He looks to see if I'm laughing at him. "I never get past the first date with a girl, and I know it's because of my breath."

I think for a moment.

This, I can do. It gives me something to focus on, something other than my life spiraling out of control. Maybe this can be my new normal. Word seems to be spreading about my new "hobby" that I inadvertently started. "I think I can help," I tell him.

We talk for another minute about what he's already tried, and then he thanks me and gives me his number.

I'll call him when I've figured out the correct recipe.

As he leaves, a handful of people enter and disperse to various parts of the store. Carla gets up from her spot and stomps over. She has tears in her eyes, and her face tightens.

"Are you still making your 'remedies'?!" Her eyes well with tears, and she looks angry. "I thought I told you that you're going to HURT someone! You have NO right to be mixing up this homemade poison for the good people of this town!"

Her face is now scarlet, and her breathing ragged. Her intensity seems out of place for a homeopathic mouth rinse.

"You need to STOP, before you hurt someone!" She storms out of the store, clothes billowing behind her.

Bill rushes to the front. "What on earth happened here?" he asks. He sounds worried.

"Carla got upset at me again," I say, sagging back against the counter.

I'm visibly shaken and trying not to cry.

"What?" he says, dumbfounded. "She did? Why?"

"She walked in on someone asking me for another homeopathic remedy, and it set her off. She was angry and said I'm poisoning people." I dab at my eye with my sleeve and then pull it down to cover my tremors.

Bill's eyes go wide. "Are you serious?"

"Totally serious," I sigh.

I don't understand why Carla is so opposed to homeopathy. I know Lilly was sick when she was young, but she said doctors gave her the wrong treatment. I'm still puzzling through how those two things overlap.

"I still don't understand why Carla is so upset. Aren't you only making, like, sleepy time tea and things like that? How would that ever hurt anyone?"

Running my fingers through my hair, I let out a deep sigh. "I don't know, Bill. It's not like it's the nineteenth century, when home remedies were made with arsenic. Maybe she's read too much about Victorian culture."

It's nearly the end of my shift, and Bill lets me go early despite being late this morning. I think he can sense that I need to calm down.

Twenty-Six

At home with Maisie in my lap, I feel steadier. Not better, but at least less shaky.

Yesterday's events have dimmed to background noise, and now I'm trying to deal with the confusing emotional fallout with Carla.

Did I do something to set her off?

I don't think so.

Why is she angry?

No idea.

Is she going to apologize again?

Doubtful.

This time feels different from the last, even though it was the same fight.

Deep down, I feel like there has to be more to this—something I don't understand.

I've always felt like Carla liked me. Yes, she's annoying. She tends to hover and chat when I'm not really interested, but I thought she was fond of me.

Have I been wrong this whole time?

Did I accidentally do something to her, maybe when I first moved here, that she hasn't forgotten, but I have?

I'm left with more questions than answers.

I feed Maisie and turn on the TV. Maybe I can get lost in mindless sitcoms for a while.

The sky darkens, and my mood remains gloomy.

Did I eat?

No, not yet.

I eat in front of the open fridge door by snacking on anything that seems edible. Pickles, a small amount of leftover cheese and half a piece of pizza from the other night.

Good enough.

Back in the living room, I lie on the floor and stare at the ceiling.

I try to clear my mind in a lazy meditation, but it's not possible.

I grab a book off the shelf. That's not working. I can't concentrate on the words and keep reading the same paragraph over and over without absorbing any of it.

I look at the time; it's 10 p.m.

When did that happen?

Maisie and I go out for her final potty break of the night. It's cold, and I cross my arms and rub them with my hands to create warmth.

I breathe out slowly and watch my breath. We didn't get a lot of cold winters growing up in California, so even after two years in Ashbourne, it's still fascinating to watch my breath freeze in front of me.

It's quiet out here tonight.

No shadows, no strange sounds.

No motion that I can't explain.

Maisie finishes up, and we go back inside to bed.

I go to the cabinet and take a sleeping pill, hoping to put the last few days out of my mind.

Between the medicine and my burnt-out nervous system, I'm asleep in no time.

I'm dreaming.

Maisie is barking.

Loud, jarring barks.

Jolting my foggy brain.

I realize I'm not asleep.

I sit up, awake, but groggy. My heart jumps. It's not quite racing yet; it's fighting the sleeping pills.

I leap out of bed, only half aware of what's happening.

Maisie is standing on the bed, still barking. Not the happy barks that I hear from the other side of the door when I come home, but deep, throaty barks that signal something isn't right, and she knows it.

Then I hear them. Loud, booming footsteps out on my porch. Whoever is out there isn't trying to be quiet; they want me to know they're here.

I throw a robe over my pajamas and rush to the front door, frantically looking out the peephole. It's too dark to see, so I flip on the porch light and try again. I can just make out someone in a black hoodie rushing down the stairs.

I stumble backwards until I find the couch and lean against it, heart racing.

Am I going to pass out?

Did I really see that?

Yes, I definitely saw something.

Rushing back to the bedroom, I grab my phone and call the police.

Ten minutes later, two officers who weren't here for the break-in the other day are asking me questions.

"What did the person look like? Was it a man or a woman? How tall were they? Fat or slim? Any defining features?"

I have no answers to their questions. All I know is that I heard Maisie barking, and then loud footsteps, followed by someone with their hood up rushing down the stairs to the street below.

They ask if I've been drinking or if I'm on any medication.

I sheepishly tell them that I took a sleeping pill, and that I had woken up to Maisie barking loudly, something she never does in the middle of the night.

The officers share a knowing glance and put their pads away.

Just as before, they tell me to call if I remember anything else, or if the perpetrator comes back.

And as quick as they were here, they're gone.

I close the door behind them and slump to the ground against it. I know they think I imagined it: the footsteps, the person in the hoodie. But I didn't.

Did I?

Could it be a hallucination?

I did wake up to Maisie barking, and the effects from the sleeping pills are strong. Is it possible that my mind is filling in blanks that aren't there?

I put my head and arms on my knees and start to cry. Not the wracking sobs that I've had plenty of lately, but big, rolling, silent tears that wet my knees.

I cry quietly, just inside the front door, trying to piece together what is real and what my mind has fabricated.

I look up again, and the faint light of sunrise is starting to peek through the trees.

I feel a cold draft from the door.

How is it morning already?

Twenty-Seven

I get up from the floor and stumble into the kitchen.

It's nearly 6 a.m. Was I asleep by the door? I don't remember.

I'm working today, but not until later, so maybe I should nap.

I lie in bed for a while, but sleep doesn't come. I stare at the ceiling and wonder what Maisie is up to. She isn't in bed with me.

I go looking for her, and she's asleep in her dog bed, snoring. Well, at least one of us is getting some shut-eye.

With no sleep in sight, I make a pot of coffee. There's no cream in the fridge, so I sip it, black, even though it's still too hot. It burns my mouth, but that doesn't stop me. I can feel the burnt skin on the roof of my mouth and on my tongue, and somehow it feels right.

I grab my tablet, thinking I'll scroll through today's headlines, but then I change my mind.

I don't need any more bad news today.

Maybe if I don't read it, it isn't real.

I decide that yoga is the best idea I've had in a couple of days, so I get in a soothing round of exercise, despite my burnt mouth. It doesn't feel right anymore.

When I'm done, I pour another cup of coffee and check my phone. I have a text from Wendy.

You ok? Worried about you. Call me.

I don't know what to do. Can I hang out with Wendy, or even talk to her? Pretend that I'm okay? That everything is normal?

I text her back.

I'm ok. You working today?

She says she isn't and wants to meet up.

I'm sweating slightly, and I swear I can smell cinnamon again. I agree we'll meet for lunch at noon, but I want to get takeout. I'm all set with being in public.

She says we can hang out at her place.

I run my hands through my hair, trying to ground myself in reality.

I'm here.

Maisie is here.

My coffee cup is half full.

Maybe last night was a half-asleep, paranoid, sleeping-pill-induced hallucination nightmare?

Were the police even really here?

Yes. They left their card.

A different officer from the other day.

I take a breath and look out the window. The sky outside is gray, but it doesn't look like rain.

I stand there for a few moments, trying to reorient myself to reality.

The sleeping pill was a terrible idea; I can't do that again. Not until things settle.

I shower and get ready to meet Wendy. The water burns my over-scrubbed skin. I turn the tap to make it hotter.

Then I'm dressed and out the door, after giving Maisie extra pets for being such a good girl.

The drive to Wendy's seems almost dreamlike. I'm numb, but hyper-aware of everything going on around me.

I pass the town center, and Carla is outside Sanderson's. She sees me, I don't know why, but I wave. She doesn't wave back.

I pull into Wendy's driveway and turn off the engine. I close my eyes and rest my head on the back of the seat. Maybe Wendy can help me.

Suddenly, there's a knock on my window. I jump and look out, but it's only Wendy, standing there, looking confused.

Only then do I notice how cold the car has gotten.

I get out, grabbing my purse and keys.

"What's going on?" she says, sounding concerned.

"What do you mean?" I ask.

"You've been sitting out here damn near 20 minutes. Did you fall asleep?" Her brows knit together. "Did you sleep last night?"

"I... don't know," I say wearily.

"You don't know what? If you were asleep out here, or if you slept last night?"

"Both," I reply as a wave of nausea grips me. Maybe it's because all I had for breakfast was coffee.

Wendy looks even more alarmed now. "Leah, what's going on? Something isn't right with you. Let's get you inside. I need you to tell me what's happening."

We trek into Wendy's house, and I instantly feel a little better. There are bright green plants in every room, making everything feel alive in a way that only plants can. All of the warm and neutral tones she's decorated with make you feel at home, even if it's your first time there.

I slump onto her couch, sinking into the throw pillows that are more comfortable than my own bed.

Wendy goes to the kitchen to get me a glass of water, and I'm asleep before she leaves the room.

Twenty-Eight

I wake sometime later, disoriented but calm. I look at the clock, and it's 6 p.m. I bolt up, panicking. "I'm going to be late for work!"

Wendy gently sits me back down. She's been watching me from a living room chair. "I called Bill and told him you weren't coming in tonight. He agreed it was a good idea. Why did you not tell me about Carla? What has been going on with you?"

I sigh. How much can I tell her?

How much will she believe? I only half believe it myself.

I start talking, and it all spills out: the voicemail, the candle, Carla, the intrusion last night.

Wendy sits, listening intently without judging me. When I finish, she moves to the couch and sits next to me, hugging me.

She loves me, I know that. In my bones, now. Even if she thinks I'm going crazy, she's here for me in a way I didn't even expect of her.

I relax into her and just let everything be.

Finally, she pulls away. "Leah, are you going to be okay? What you've been through would be a lot for anyone." She rests her hand gently on my shoulder.

"I don't know anymore, Wendy. I feel like I'm going crazy. I'm not sure what is real. I'm losing time. I sat at my door last night after the police left around 1 a.m., but suddenly it was almost six. I don't think I slept." I start to cry, and she hugs me again until it subsides.

"Something I don't really understand, what's up with the voicemail? Why is an old news broadcast so scary?" She looks at me questioningly.

I grab my phone and put it on speaker.

... following the failed ChemGen clinical trial that left multiple people injured, and several in critical condition...

"Well, that's creepy," Wendy says with a slight shiver.

I sigh and fall back against the couch cushions. "It's not only creepy, it's me. It's about the clinical trial that ended my career." I let out a sigh of relief. Wendy is the first person I've told about this in years.

Her eyes open wide, and she sucks in a breath. "Oh my God! Are you serious? How on earth would someone have access to an old news broadcast from California? I thought you said that your career ended because of a disagreement with corporate?"

I look at her solemnly. "I don't know how someone found this clip from a news broadcast, but I haven't told you everything, Wendy."

She nods. She knew that when we briefly discussed my background last week, I hadn't gone into detail because it was too painful. She waits, not wanting to push me before I'm ready.

"I was the lead scientist on a clinical trial for a drug called NVX-201. It was an anagen therapy we developed to treat autoimmune neural atrophy. It's rare." I look up, and she shakes her head. It's not a disease she's aware of.

"Well, it's a genetic autoimmune disorder that, if left untreated, causes progressive paralysis that eventually extends to the whole body, including the vocal cords. It's terrible."

I sigh, knowing that what I have to tell her next is the hardest part. "Like I said, it was doing well in animal trials, and the results were excellent. The board insisted we move to human clinical trials, when I wasn't sure the drug was ready.

"The data looked great, but there wasn't enough of it to support moving to human trials so quickly. I never understood the rush." I look down, trying to suppress the emotions swelling within me.

I haven't talked about this in so long, and it feels like a freight train leaving my body. It's a weight lifted, but not without internal damage. "They gave me a choice: start the trials, or I would be fired. And sure, it seems easy to 'just find a new job,' but it isn't as simple as that. I would have been blacklisted from every major biotech company on the west coast, and probably most of the east too." I look up.

Wendy is listening intently but doesn't ask any questions. She's patiently waiting for me to finish my story on my own terms.

"So, I made the wrong choice. I approved the trial. People got hurt, and even years later, I still can't forgive myself." A tear rolls down my cheek, and then another.

Wendy hugs me and lets me cry.

Finally, the tears dry up, and I switch gears back to my current problem. "But all of this, the voicemail, the break-in, the footsteps last night. It all feels connected. I don't know if someone from my past is trying to scare me, or if they're here for retribution."

My eyes fill with tears again, but they don't fall. "The candle and the smaller things can all be explained away by me being a hyper-vigilant psycho about my safety and could be nothing. But I feel like things are escalating. Could it really be someone out for revenge?"

Wendy has been quiet until now. "Leah, this wasn't your fault." She looks me directly in the eye. "The data looked good, and you built your entire career on being a smart and calculated scientist."

"It absolutely *is* my fault. I knew that we needed more data, and I approved it anyway. Sure, it was under duress, but I still made the wrong call. If I had walked away, I would have lost everything, but I lost everything regardless. And now I get to carry the guilt with me for the rest of my life."

Wendy knows I'm right. "Okay, but what about the board?"

I flinch. "The company was forced to shut down its pharmaceutical division, but it didn't go under. They're still around, actually. They were recently bought out and are reopening that side of the business."

"Wow." Wendy sounds shocked. "I am so sorry. I wish there were something, anything, I could do to help."

"It's okay. It was years ago now. I do miss it, but honestly, the homeopathic remedies I'm seemingly becoming known for here have filled a gap that I didn't even realize was there. It's brought me an almost bittersweet joy to be back at my roots."

I tell her about Nan, about growing up around herbs and tinctures and salves, about the warmth of my childhood in her garden and kitchen.

"I had no idea," Wendy says. "She sounds wonderful." She looks at the clock. "You know what, let's have something to eat." Wendy breaks up my spiraling by suggesting food. It's a great idea.

"What are we having?" I ask.

She smiles. "Leftover Chinese. I'll reheat the food I bought for lunch, since it's dinner time now."

In no time, we're sitting at her kitchen table eating hot food. I try to remember the last meal I ate, but I can't.

This is soothing. Calming in a way that I haven't felt in days now. I'm safe with Wendy. Not just physically, but emotionally.

Wendy twirls noodles around a fork and pops them into her mouth. "You're not staying at home tonight," she says with her mouth full. "You're staying here." A stray noodle falls back into her plate.

I balk. "I can't! I can't leave Maisie all alone. I wouldn't do that to her."

"Ah, I forgot about Maisie." She thinks for a minute. "That's no problem, Maisie can stay here too."

"Are you sure?" I ask. The last place I want to be tonight is home alone with Maisie, but I also don't want to impose.

"Um, of course!" she says. "Without question. There isn't a chance I'm letting you be alone right now."

"Thank you," I say quietly into my egg roll.

Twenty-Nine

After we eat, Wendy drives me back to my place, and I pack a bag for myself and Maisie. I check to make sure the candle is out, just in case.

Maisie is so excited to go on a car ride; she doesn't care where we're going. We roll the window down enough for her to get her nose out, even though it's cold. She's such a good dog; she deserves a little fun.

When we get to Wendy's, she leaps out of the car, runs right up to the front door and sits on the stoop. You'd think she lived here, and it wasn't her first time.

After Maisie checks out the whole house, sniffing every inch so as not to miss a single new scent, she lies down on her dog bed for a nap.

Wendy and I are relaxing on the couch, a glass of wine in hand. I feel better, safer than I have in days. She has a home security system and cameras that record the front and back of the house, something I always wished I could afford.

We moved on hours ago from the conversations about all the awful things that have been happening, and it's been comforting to talk about nearly meaningless subjects again.

The guy she was dating turned out to be a walking red flag, so that's over. She says she may be single for the rest of her life.

I doubt that. She's smart, gorgeous, funny and kind.

Her washing machine broke, so she laments about the cost of buying a new one.

I wish I had a washing machine.

Sitting here, conversing about the completely mundane, is so refreshing that I can feel it healing me.

The conversation turns to my hiking trip the other day.

Wendy looks surprised. "You hung out with Mina? Did you ever end up learning more about her?" She tilts her head sideways as if she's trying to determine if I'm serious, and then takes a sip of wine.

I had forgotten entirely, with everything going on, to ask Wendy about her past with Mina. "I've actually hung out with her several times now. The first time I ran into her was on my way back from the lake. I was walking with Maisie, and she was out taking nature photographs. She's actually pretty good. We walked back to town together."

Wendy seems surprised but doesn't comment. She lets me continue.

"The second time, I ran into her at the grocery store, and we ended up grabbing coffee and then talking in the car for a couple of hours at The Point."

Now she looks shocked. "You went with a *stranger*, in her car, to a remote place to talk? Leah, maybe you actually are going crazy."

I blush. I know she's right. "Yeah, I don't really know how it happened. I rationalized it because we walked back from the woods together. If she had wanted to hurt me, wouldn't that have been the best opportunity? Remote place, nobody around?" I realize how flimsy that excuse sounds now.

Wendy nods at me to continue my story, but her eyebrows still convey her surprise.

"The last time was Saturday. I woke up, and it was such a beautiful day. I wanted to go hiking. I know you hate hiking, so I didn't bother texting you. She's the only other person I really know here, and I again rationalized that she'd already had two opportunities to hurt me and didn't. So I texted her, and off we went."

Wendy is floored. She sits back against the arm of the couch, speechless. To her, this is probably the most unhinged thing I've said today. For as long as she's known me, I've avoided other people like the plague. Now, I've been complicit in making a new friend.

"I know, I know," I say. "It sounds like I've lost my mind, but for some reason I can't really explain, I trust her." I take a sip of wine and wait a moment for it all to sink in.

"So." I clear my throat. "She also told me about growing up here. Supposedly, you grew up together."

Wendy's brows touch again. "I didn't grow up with a 'Mina'," she replies.

"I know, but did you grow up with a Wilhemina, who went by 'Willa'?" I ask her.

Her eyes open wide again. "Oh, yes! I knew Willa. We were both friends with Megan. She changed her name?" She stirs her wine with a finger.

"She did. Apparently, she wasn't well-liked as a kid, and she changed her name in college to distance herself from some bullying." I'm hoping that Wendy will offer more context on their shared childhood.

"Oh, interesting. Good for her. She was always nice, but she was a little weird in school. Shy, tall, lanky. Just all around awkward, you know? What does she do now? Married? Kids?"

Wendy is genuinely interested in how Mina is doing as an adult. I should have known; she has no idea the damage she caused to Mina when they were kids. It definitely wasn't intentional.

"She's in crisis management now. I guess she travels all over for work, but she visits Ashbourne pretty regularly to take care of her parents. They had her late in life, so they're older and not in great health." I'm still searching

Wendy's eyes for a sign that she knew what she was doing back then. I really don't think she did.

She picks up on me trying to study her reaction. "What?" she asks, confused.

"You don't realize the part you played in her being miserable here, do you?" I say it gently. I'm not trying to antagonize the only friend I have that I'm sure I can trust.

"Excuse me?" she's annoyed. "What are you talking about? I was never mean to Willa. I mean, 'Mina'. I never made fun of her or put her down. Did she say that? That I bullied her?"

Wendy spends her life caring for others, so the thought that someone might accuse her of hurting them is completely unfathomable to her.

"No, Wendy. She didn't say you bullied her."

She relaxes slightly, but I can tell she's still agitated. "Well then, what DID she say?"

I sigh. "I'm not trying to argue with you or accuse you of anything. I know you're a good person, and I know that you were probably a good person even back then, when other people were teenage shits. She didn't accuse you of bullying her, but she says you never stood up for her. You never tried to stop other people from bullying her, despite having some of the same friends."

Wendy is astonished. "We were *ten*. What was I supposed to do? I have no idea what she expected of me, but I was a kid. I didn't participate in the bullying. I never said an unkind word to her."

"Did you ever say a kind one?" I ask gently. "Or did you pretend she didn't exist because her situation was uncomfortable to be a part of?"

Wendy opens her mouth to speak, then closes it again. She puts her hand to her head as if suppressing a headache. "You know what, Leah, I need a few minutes."

She gets up off the couch, goes into her bedroom and shuts the door.

Have I broken the only good relationship I've had in years?

I wonder how badly I've screwed up.

Thirty

I'm lying in the guest bed, Maisie asleep at my side. I feel terrible about Wendy's reaction.

But knowing Mina's side, I had to say something. The way Mina tenses up when she talks about her childhood, and the sadness in her voice when she mentions the places around Ashbourne, is tangible. It obviously still haunts her. If Wendy could realize that just because she wasn't the villain doesn't mean she's the hero, maybe she and Mina could reconcile.

I roll over. I'm grateful to Wendy for letting me stay here, especially after I called her out right after all her kindness towards Maisie and me.

I'm not scared, but this house is different than my apartment. I hear the furnace kick on and the dishwasher running.

Wendy's air freshener smells like vanilla and sandalwood. She buys nice sheets, so the high-thread-count cotton is both soft and cool on my skin.

I finally feel safe and comfortable, but I'm miserable. For myself, for Mina, for Wendy. For the clinical trial in my past. For Nan.

Oh, what I wouldn't give to hear Nan's voice again. She sounds like aging velvet. Soft, warm and silky all at once.

I hear a knock at the bedroom door, and I bolt upright, hand to my heart.

"Leah?" Wendy sounds muffled through the door. "Can I come in?"

"Of course," I say, forcing myself to breathe again. I hadn't expected to see her tonight; I figured we'd talk in the morning.

She opens the door, walks in, and sits at the foot of the bed. "I'm sorry for how I reacted tonight. I had no idea Mina felt that way when we were kids. I wish she had said something." Her eyes are swollen like she's been crying.

I get out of bed and sit beside her, wrapping her in a hug. "Wendy, I never meant to make you feel like this. I know you were just a kid. I'm so sorry."

She shakes her head. "You're right, though. I have some soul-searching to do. Do you mind if I sleep in here with you and Maisie?"

I smile. "Get in."

We curl up together, and it's the most peaceful I've felt in weeks, maybe years.

I fall asleep almost instantly.

We wake up the next morning, make coffee and have breakfast. Wendy doesn't mess around with her meals. There are pancakes, bacon, eggs, sausages, toast and fruit salad.

We avoid Mina as a topic of conversation, and I think that's for the best right now.

"I have to work this morning," Wendy tells me. "What about you?"

"Yeah, I have to work too, but not until noon today." I'm glad I don't have to be out the door too soon.

"I've been thinking," Wendy says, biting a sausage, then taking a sip of coffee. "I don't know how crazy this sounds, but maybe you should move in here for a while."

I'm stunned. My mouth hangs open, and egg falls back onto my plate. "What?"

Wendy looks at me and sighs. "Yeah, I know it's nuts. But wouldn't you feel better being here? I know I'd feel better about it. It doesn't have to be permanent, only until the dust settles." She waits for my response.

"I... I don't know, Wendy. That's a pretty big favor you'd be doing us. And what about all of my things?"

Wendy laughs. "You have, like, *maybe* four boxes of things, plus your bed. You can store them in the garage till you figure out what you're going to do later. And it's not a huge favor. I live here alone, it would be nice to have a roommate, and I love Maisie."

My mind races. "Can we talk about it later? It's a selfless offer, but I want to give you time to change your mind. It's a lot. *I'm* a lot." I don't want to overextend Wendy's kindness.

Wendy smiles. "It's true, you are a lot. But you're my best friend, and I need to make sure you're okay." She goes back to eating breakfast like it's her job.

Before Wendy leaves for work, we agree that Maisie and I will stay again tonight, and we'll talk over the logistics of possibly moving in.

Maisie and I take a drive over to our apartment to pick up a few more things. We do a quick grocery run to stock Wendy's fridge, both as a thank-you and because we may be staying there for a while.

We go back to Wendy's house, and I take Maisie for a quick walk around the neighborhood. It's only a 10-minute drive from the town center, but it's peaceful. A beautiful, tree-lined street, with other houses in view but not so close you can see into their backyards.

In the spring, there is wildlife: birds chirping and deer in the woods. It's a lovely place to be, and I consider again what it may be like to live here with Wendy.

After a quick shower and a sandwich, it's time to go to work. The drive to Sanderson's is serene but significantly longer than the drive from my apartment. That's one negative, though a small one.

The store is steady for a Wednesday. Several large purchases create a line at the register for a short time, but I clear them as quickly as possible. Stocking and cleaning are welcome tasks compared to my last few days, and I'm just glad to be back in a routine.

Carla comes into the store briefly, but she doesn't engage with me. When Brad relieves me from the register, she makes a purchase and then leaves without looking in my direction.

It's a welcome change from the other day. I'd rather she not speak to me at all than have her scream at me.

I'm wiping down the beer case when I hear my name. I tense and turn around slowly.

It's Mina.

"Oh, hey!" I say, putting down the rag and wiping my hands on my pants. "How are you?"

"I'm fine," she replies. "My parents needed a few things, and I didn't feel like driving all the way to FoodMart. How's work going?"

"Work is great!" I say, a little too enthusiastically.

Mina smiles at my weirdness. "Glad to hear it."

We make small talk for a few minutes while I finish wiping down the case, and then I move to the large shelf in the back that holds two-gallon glass jugs of wine. I have to dust them once a week, or they start to look like something out of a horror movie.

She doesn't seem too eager to go back to her parents' house. "What are you up to later?"

"Oh, just hanging at Wendy's tonight," I tell her. I'm not ready to start announcing that we may move in together. Especially since it makes me look like a leech.

"Again? Nice, sounds fun," she says, distracted by a customer coming in the door.

Weird, I think. Did I tell her I'd stayed at Wendy's last night?

She turns back and meets my eyes, and her expression slips momentarily. Almost like she realized she said something she shouldn't have. It happens so fast, I could have imagined it, and she's smiling again.

"So, a girl's night?" she asks, her smile broad and genuine.

I must have imagined it. I had to have said something when we were chatting earlier.

"Yeah, sort of." I give an awkward laugh. I don't know her well enough to confide everything in her like I have with Wendy. "Just with the break-in, and then I thought I heard footsteps the other night... Wendy's looking out for me."

Mina's smile wanes, and she looks stricken. "Another intruder?"

I freeze. As much as I like Mina, I don't want to confide all of my problems and rehash my issues with her. At least not yet. "Yeah, maybe... I'm not sure."

Sensing my hesitation, she changes the subject. "I'm really glad Wendy's been there for you like she has." I can tell she really doesn't like to think about Wendy.

I'm up on the top step of the ladder now, trying to dust the bottles at the back of the shelf. They're the ones that everyone else pretends don't exist, so they're only dusted when I do it.

"Be careful!" Mina says, sounding concerned. "That shelf doesn't look very stable."

"Don't worry," I tell her. "It's anchored to the wall. With all the heavy bottles on here, it would be a lawsuit waiting to happen." I stand on my tiptoes to reach the very back of the highest shelf, grabbing the side for support. As I'm dusting the last bottle, I feel the ladder shift underneath me, and the case starts to tip forward.

I'm falling. I hit the ground a second before a dozen glass jugs slide off the shelves, smashing all around me.

Thirty-One

There's a ringing in my ears, and the smell of blood and wine is all around me. For a minute, I don't know where I am.

Is this Wendy's house?

I see gray hair. "Nan?" I realize that doesn't make sense. Nan is on the other side of the country. "Bill?"

"Shhhh, it's going to be okay," Bill says tenderly. "You had a fall. The ambulance is on the way."

"What?" I don't understand.

Where did I fall from?

Bill turns to Mina. "Can you go with her in the ambulance, or should I?"

I've mentioned hanging out with her in passing, so he knows we're friends.

The world around me is blurry, and Bill sounds like he's underwater.

"I can go," Mina replies. "I'm not squeamish at all."

Underwater Bill sounds relieved. "Okay, great," he says. "I'm going to have to close the store today to get a cleanup company to come out for the blood. There are laws about that, you know."

Mina doesn't say anything. She must have replied without words.

Suddenly, there's commotion around me, and someone is lifting me onto a stretcher. My vision has cleared a little. I look at the floor, and it's covered in glass, blood and wine.

Who made that mess?

I hear Mina talking to the EMTs. "She was up on that ladder, and it folded just as the shelf tipped. All six of the jugs from the top fell on her, and two hit her on the head."

So, I made this mess? The last thing I remember is dusting the bottles at the back.

One of the paramedics asks me my name and what day it is.

"Ellie," I say automatically. Wait, no. That's not my name. "No... Leah. Ellie was my family nickname." I miss my family.

"What day is it?"

"Is it Monday?" I feel like it is, but I'm not sure.

The same paramedic turns to Mina to say it sounds like a concussion and asks if she wants to ride in the ambulance.

She says she's coming with us.

I'm glad. I don't want to be alone at the hospital. I don't know how bad it is, but if it's bad, I'm glad Mina will be there with me.

I try to ask her to call Wendy, but my voice doesn't sound right.

"Shhh, it's going to be okay. Let's get you checked out before you start reciting Shakespeare, okay?"

Despite my injuries and confusion, I smile. Mina is a good friend.

The paramedics load me into the ambulance, and Mina sits near my head, leaning down to hold my hand. She gives it a squeeze every once in a while.

One of the EMTs takes my vitals and then periodically asks me my name, who the president is or what month or year it is.

I get most of them right.

I feel sleepy. The medic tells me I have to stay awake, and now I'm grumpy. It's been such a stressful few days. I don't really remember why, though. I know I stayed at Wendy's for a couple of nights. Did I tell her about the clinical trial? No, that doesn't sound right. I wouldn't have done that.

I'm not sure how long we drove for, but now we're at the ER, and they're wheeling me in through a special entrance. The medics talk briefly with the charge nurse, and I'm wheeled into a large room that is divided into sections by very outdated curtains.

Mina is gone briefly, and then she's at my side. "I spoke with the head nurse; they're going to do an exam and then probably a CT scan. The cuts you have are all surface-level, thankfully. I was really concerned because it looked like a lot of blood, but they're not serious. I also called Wendy; she'll be here soon."

That's right, I asked her to call Wendy. I must have given her Wendy's number on the way here.

The doctor comes in and does a neurological exam. He says I definitely have a concussion, but they need to do imaging to see how bad it is.

Now he's gone, but a nurse is taking my temperature again. The thermometer is cold.

Why do my feet feel like ice?

Mina is on the phone. She looks concerned and is nodding. "Okay, thanks, Bill," she says.

Why is her voice so loud? Do these curtains amplify sound? I can hear the nurse taking someone's blood pressure three bays away.

She hangs up and looks at me with concern. "How are you doing, Leah? They should be by soon to get you for the CT scan." She puts her hand over mine.

It's comforting. I'm glad she's here.

What's that noise? Oh, Wendy is here now, too.

Why does it feel like all the oxygen has been sucked out of the room?

"God, Leah, are you okay?!" Wendy has tears in her eyes, and she's replaced Mina by my side. "What happened?"

I start to answer, but the words still aren't coming out quite right.

Thankfully, Mina takes over and starts to fill Wendy in.

I hear a gasp from Wendy as she learns that both the ladder slipped, and the jugs fell on me. "How did that happen?" Wendy asks.

Mina glances at me and squirms, unsure if she should say what she's about to say. "I talked to Bill, and the anchor that held the shelf to the wall had been cut."

Cut? Did I hear her right? I'm shaking, and I'm not sure if it's from Mina's words or the chill in the room.

I'm starting to remember the fall, but everything hurts now.

My head aches, the light hurts, and even my teeth.

"The police are checking it out, but it's going to be hard to prove someone did it. Bill has a few cameras in the shop, but they're mostly pointed at the area around the register. The single camera pointed in that direction didn't pick up anything helpful." Mina sighs and runs her fingers through her hair.

Wendy looks dumbfounded. "Do you think they were trying to kill Leah? I mean, it could have been anyone on that ladder cleaning the shelves. Could it have been a prank gone wrong?"

I can hear the disbelief in Wendy's voice as she tries to wrap her head around this situation.

Just then, a nurse arrives with a wheelchair to take me to my scan. I'm back within 20 minutes, and Wendy and Mina appear to be sitting awkwardly in my bay, looking at their phones without interacting.

The nurse helps me back into the small hospital bed and tells me the doctor should be around soon with my results.

I can feel my head starting to clear up, at least a little.

I'm sore, but less confused than I was. My speech has mostly returned to normal. "What's going on in here, tech time?" I joke, trying to lighten the mood.

Wendy and Mina both smile, but it's more polite than happy.

"How are you feeling?" they both ask at the same time. Looking at each other, they laugh awkwardly.

"I'm a little better," I say. "When we left the store, I could hardly understand what was going on. Things are still a little foggy, and it's almost like time has slowed down. But I'm pretty sure that the report is going to say I'm okay to go home."

Wendy and Mina both look relieved. Mina speaks first. "I'm glad to hear that you're feeling slightly better. It was really scary watching you fall; it seemed to happen in slow motion." She lets out a breath like she's been holding it for hours.

"I'll stay here as long as they keep you, and you'll come home with me, at the very least until you're better." It's not a request from Wendy, it's a demand.

I smile at my best friend. "Thank you."

Mina shifts, looking a little uncomfortable. "I'm going to stay until you get your results, and then I'm going to head home for the night." She looks at Wendy, almost tentatively. "Thanks for letting her stay with you. I don't think it's safe for her to be home alone right now."

Wendy meets her gaze. "Of course, I wouldn't have it any other way. Especially since we don't even know if she's being targeted."

Mina's face turns serious. "I think it's best to assume she is. Plan for the worst, hope for the best."

"I'm certainly not taking any chances." Wendy looks back at her phone. I think she's so uncomfortable because of our conversation the other night, and I feel bad for even bringing it up.

The doctor arrives and tells me there is no sign of bleeding on the imaging. It's a mild concussion, and I'm very lucky. Over the next couple of days, I'll probably feel groggy, sensitive to light, have a headache, and have difficulty focusing. I can expect gradual improvement over the next seven to ten days, but I need to make sure not to push myself too hard, or symptoms can return.

We breathe a collective sigh of relief, and Wendy hugs me. Mina tells me she's glad I'm going to be okay, and that she'll text me tomorrow, squeezing my hand on her way out.

I have to stay for a few more hours for monitoring, but then Wendy and I can go home. I can't wait to take a nap; I'm exhausted.

Wendy gets up to use the bathroom, and a moment later, a nurse comes in with paperwork. I assume it's the discharge papers, so I ask if we can wait until Wendy is back.

"Well, hon, this isn't actually about your discharge. There seems to be an insurance issue." She looks at me kindly, as if she knows this is the last thing I need right now.

I look at her questioningly. "What's the problem?"

"Your insurance is claiming there's a social security number/name mismatch issue. I'm sure that it's a technical problem on their end, but once you're feeling better, you'll have to call and sort it out. Otherwise, you're going to get a pretty hefty bill."

"Ugh," I groan. This isn't the first time this has happened. You would think that when you call to fix a problem, they'd fix it for good, not just for one claim. "Thank you for letting me know. It's a known issue, and I can get it resolved in the next day or two."

She thanks me and scoots back out. Wendy is walking back in at the same time. "Hey, were those your discharge instructions? I want to talk to her before we leave." She looks annoyed that they showed up while she was gone for five minutes.

I roll my eyes. "No, just an insurance issue. It's not a problem; I'll get it cleared up as soon as I'm feeling well enough to argue with the insurance company."

We wait another 30 minutes, and the nurse returns with discharge instructions. Rest, monitoring by another adult for the next 24 hours, acetaminophen for pain, and watch for warning signs that things are worsening. They give us the paperwork with a list of symptoms to look out for.

Wendy pulls the car around, and the nurse wheels me out to her idling vehicle.

I carefully get into the passenger seat. The car is warm and comforting.

It's just after 9 p.m., and the darkness is a welcome change for my throbbing head. I briefly smell cinnamon, and then I'm asleep.

Thirty-Two

Bill gives me the week off from work to rest and recover. He tells me he's going to pay me for the leave, and I try to argue, but he insists. I'm grateful because I know I can't get by on air, and I'm currently still paying rent at my place.

Staying with Wendy feels like being in a safe house. With her alarms and cameras, I actually *do* feel safe, something I haven't felt in a very long time.

I spend the first two days truly recovering; I barely leave the guest bedroom except to let Maisie out or use the bathroom.

I sleep. Deep sleep, the kind you only get when you aren't waiting for the next nightmare. I dream of Nan, of Maisie running through a field, of Wendy hiking with me. I have blurred, confusing dreams of Mina, Brad, Carla and Bill, but not nightmares. I even have a dream about Pete where he's wearing dirty overalls, and he's okay with it.

On day three, I start leaving the room, napping less and cleaning the house more. If I'm staying here, I want to contribute in any way I can.

On day four, I make breakfast and dinner, and even do some yoga.

It's now day five, and I'm feeling significantly better. Things get a little foggy sometimes, but my headaches have mostly subsided, and the sensitivity to light is thankfully gone.

I'm going to take Maisie for a proper walk today, around this beautiful neighborhood.

I made breakfast, did yoga and cleaned the bathroom, so I've already contributed to the house and invested in myself.

Now it's Maisie's turn. I get her leash, and she's practically leaping into my arms to show her excitement.

It's a chilly day, but the sun is shining, and it feels good to be outside. Maisie and I are exploring Wendy's neighborhood, possibly *our* new neighborhood. It's mostly single-family homes, complete with white picket fences and hybrid SUVs in the driveways. It's the type of neighborhood you'd choose to raise a family.

The route I picked should be a mild walk, about half an hour. I didn't want to plan too aggressively or overdo it, but I also wanted to reward Maisie for being such a great houseguest. She's adjusted wonderfully and hasn't left us any unwelcome surprises.

A car whizzes past, going too fast for a suburban neighborhood.

We come up behind a mom pushing a stroller. I smile at her and say hello as we pass.

We are nearly back when I glance at the tree line and see a shimmer. It's a quick, pale flash. I'm reminded of the walk at the lake with Mina and her camera, but Mina isn't here now.

I don't see it again before we get back to the house.

By day seven, I'm ready to go back to work.

Sure, it was nice to get a week to recover, but I'm driving myself crazy hanging around the house.

Stocking shelves and cashing out customers used to feel dull, but it's a welcome comfort in my now somehow stranger life.

It's Tuesday, and it's been a week since my "accident."

The police uncovered nothing that confirmed foul play.

The wall anchor was plastic and appeared to have snapped or been cut. It was only four feet off the ground, so that left no leads.

The ladder was written off as a total accident.

No leads means nobody to question.

Maybe it was an accident, but I don't know what to believe.

I walk into Sanderson's at noon for a five-hour shift. Bill insisted on starting me slowly to make sure I'm okay. I'm very grateful for Bill; he's turned out to be more of a friend than I ever could have imagined.

He tells Brad that I'm on the register for this shift and that he doesn't want me stocking shelves or cleaning.

Brad grumbles but accepts the less favorable tasks. Maybe his psychology classes are actually starting to pay off.

Bill has also scheduled Brianna from noon to five. He rarely schedules three of us, but he says that he wants me to be able to go home if I need to.

My shift is mostly quiet: checking out customers, keeping the counter clean and stocking only the items behind it, like cigarettes and scratch tickets.

I ask Brad to take the register, and I pop out back to check on Bill. We didn't talk all week because I wasn't at work.

He says he's been good, but he got a new phone, and he doesn't know how to use it.

It's Bill's first smartphone.

I show him the basics of making a call and sending a text. Then I ask if he's interested in social media.

"Ahh, I don't know, Leah. I'm an old guy, and I don't understand a lot of this new technology. Is social media worth learning?" He scratches his head as if I've asked him to perform brain surgery.

"Well, it might be a good idea to create a page for the store at least. You could take pictures and post about sales, specials and new items we have. You could run holiday promotions to bring in more tourists. It would be an excellent way to get free marketing."

Bill looks bewildered but agrees to let me help him with a page for the store.

I promise that I'll get him up and running and teach him what he needs to know to keep it going.

It will be a nice distraction for me and something to do other than work and hang out with Wendy.

I make my way back out front so I'm not leaving all the work for Brad and Brianna, but between customers, I start setting up Sanderson's social media page. Once it's done, I'll teach Bill how to work it and add new pictures. It will be nice for him to have something other than his paintings to do, something he can maintain.

It's nearly lunchtime when Carla enters the store. She avoids me and goes the long way to the sitting area, Lilly in tow. She corners Brianna and chats with her for a while, the way she used to with me.

I'm grateful that she has turned her attention away from me, but I feel bad that Brianna had to take my place.

When Carla finally seems to sense Brianna's discomfort, she takes her leave and goes to the bathroom. A few minutes later, she emerges and reenters the sitting area, but Lilly is no longer there. She searches the store's aisles, and not seeing Lilly anywhere, starts to panic, her voice rising with each iteration of "Lilly! Where are you? LILLY!"

As the rest of us begin to help search for her, Lilly comes out of the bathroom.

"I'm here, Mom. I'm sorry, I thought you saw me go in when you left." She looks at the floor.

Carla drops to the floor, dramatically cradling Lilly's face to her chest. "Oh my God, Lilly, you scared me SO much. Don't ever do that again." Tears pour down her beet-red face, and she's breathing hard like she just finished a 500-yard dash.

I feel bad for Carla. I can't imagine spending my life with that kind of worry.

If I'm honest with myself, though, I *do* live with that kind of worry, just not about someone else.

I'm extremely glad I don't have kids because it seems even more emotionally debilitating.

Carla gets up, still clutching her daughter, and moves toward the door. She looks up and glares at me as she passes, as if I'm somehow responsible for Lilly needing the restroom.

Lilly looks at me blankly, as if disassociating is how she deals with her overprotective mother.

I sit back down at the counter, glad that they're gone. These days, Carla is an energy vampire. Every room she enters seems to lose a few degrees of heat and zap me of the strength I'm rebuilding.

A few minutes later, I'm in the break room getting ready to eat lunch.

I pop into Bill's office to show him what I've done so far with Sanderson's social media page, and he seems delighted. He can't wait for me to show him how to operate it.

Finally, I sit down to eat my sandwich. I'm scrolling headlines on my phone today because I've gotten out of the habit.

Really, my entire morning routine is different now that I'm staying with Wendy.

I take a bite, and something sharp pokes into the roof of my mouth. "Ow!" I pull away and taste blood.

Something small and silver is sticking out of the bread.

The world condenses, squeezing the air out of my chest.

Whatever it is appears to be metal.

I peel apart the sandwich and see a small piece of thin wire coiled around itself. The ends are razor sharp.

I push back in my chair, shocked.

How did this happen? I packed my lunch myself this morning.

Who could have been back here unseen?

It's my first day back; am I not even safe at work anymore?

I grab my phone and use the camera to see the wound. It's tiny and only slightly bleeding now. The area around it is sore, like a bruise.

I pull the wire out of my sandwich and examine it. It's about three inches long, very thin, but sturdy. It rolls in my fingers, and only the two ends are sharp enough to hurt someone.

Nobody has been back here except Brad and Brianna. Maybe Bill. But I honestly don't think any of them would have done this.

I don't think it's possible for a customer to slip by the register unnoticed.

My observant nature is what's kept me on edge for years now. Just about nothing gets by me.

The world is still squeezing me, tighter than it has in over a week.

I call Wendy, but it goes to voicemail. She's at work and probably busy. I think about texting Mina, but even though she was there for me the night of my fall, I still don't think we're close enough to call her for comfort.

I know I'm spiraling. I need to get out of here.

I tell Bill that I'm not feeling well and that the day may have been more than I can handle.

It's true, but only because of the wire. He tells me to go home, rest and take the next day off, that we'll try again on Thursday.

He asks if I can stop by for an hour tomorrow if I'm feeling up to it. He wants to learn how to update his social media, and he's really excited about it.

I smile tiredly and tell him I will absolutely stop by and give him a tutorial.

As I'm walking out of the store, I see Carla and Lilly standing on the corner talking to a group of people. Carla has an angry expression. She looks up, sees me and gestures in my direction.

She's obviously talking about me.

I'm trying my best not to care, but everything from the last few weeks, the break-in, footsteps, the candle, the voicemail, the fall, the rumors, the wire, all come crashing down around me.

I sink to the ground in front of Sanderson's in complete despair.

The doctor said emotional volatility could be a symptom of the concussion.

Is that what this is? Or is my emotional spiral right now valid?

I need to talk to someone. I need the comfort of a voice that I know I can trust.

Getting up, I make a decision.

I walk one street over to the phone repair shop. I've never been in here before, but the atmosphere is what you'd expect. Minimal décor, a counter with a spectacled man working away on a computer, too-bright fluorescent lights and a few racks of computer and phone-related goods for sale. I think they'll have what I'm looking for.

I approach the counter, and the man looks at me over the top of his glasses. "Can I help you?" he says as if I'm interrupting him.

"Yes, hi," I say with more confidence than I feel. "Do you sell prepaid cell phones?"

The man looks at me, interested. I can see him studying me. My face, my clothes, my frame, wondering what I need a burner phone for.

He uses his glasses to point. "Yes, we have a few; they're over there on that display case." He can't make a judgment based on my appearance, so he goes back to working on the computer.

"Thanks," I say, with a little less confidence. I walk over to the case and see a few types. I only need one for a few minutes, so I buy the cheapest one they carry—60 minutes, good for 30 days.

The man studies me again, then rings up my purchase and bags it. He goes back to his computer.

My story has lost his attention. That's fine by me.

I drive back to Wendy's house, where I sit with Maisie on the floor, stroking her and trying to erase today from my mind. It doesn't work, of course.

After taking her out, we sit together on Wendy's couch as I contemplate whether I'm actually going to make this phone call. I think again about everything that has happened.

Note. Voicemail. Break-in. Candle. Footsteps. Shelf. Wire.

All the times I've felt watched; the times that something unsettled me, but I couldn't put my finger on it. All of it has morphed into something bigger than me, like a monster in my closet that I know is growing, day by day, waiting for the right moment to rip me apart.

I open the burner phone and stare at it a moment, realizing that making this choice could change everything.

Maybe I need to change everything.

I dial the number I've known by heart since I was a child. It rings twice and then picks up.

"Hello?" Her voice is a beautiful lilt that pierces through my fear and anxiety.

"Nan?" It's the only word I get out before dissolving into tears.

"Ellie?" She sounds shocked to hear my voice on the other end of the line. "Ellie, my child, are you okay? What's wrong?"

Her concern makes everything worse because I know I can't tell her what's wrong.

Everything is wrong.

"Nan, I... I just needed to hear your voice. I miss my life, I miss home." I'm crying now, sobbing into the phone.

I can hear that she's trying to comfort me, but I can't make out the words over my own sobs.

"Ellie," she says again, "take a breath. Breathe in, breathe out. Deep breaths, now."

She manages to calm me, even from thousands of miles away. I know she's right. Breathing correctly has always been my coping mechanism; it's something she taught me before I even learned to walk.

"Whatever is going on, child, you need to stay calm. Are you safe right now?" I can hear the deep concern in her voice.

I look around Wendy's house. "Yes, Nan. Right now I'm safe." It's only a half-truth, but I can't burden her with everything else.

"Oh, my dear Ellie, I miss you so much. Please always know: if you find your way home, you will find your way forward. It's the only way you'll ever find peace."

I can hear the sadness that's crept into her tone, knowing she may never see me again, knowing this may be the last time we ever hear each other's voices.

"Thank you for picking up the phone, Nan. I have to go. I love you."

The tears are still rolling down my cheeks, but I know I can't keep her, no matter how much I want to.

"Always, my Ellie. Always."

I say goodbye and hang up. Then I take Maisie, and we go for an hour drive outside of Ashbourne, and I smash the phone on the ground before throwing it away in a dumpster behind a drug store.

I'm numb. I don't feel better. If anything, talking to Nan for a few minutes somehow made everything worse.

I can't ever find my way home, Nan knows that much. I've been stuck in this cycle for years, and even if things are worse right now than they've been, there is no home or moving forward for me.

I'm trapped in this awful life that I've created, and it's nobody's fault but my own.

Thirty-Three

I wake the next morning feeling hungover, even though I hadn't had a drink or taken anything the night before.

My headache has returned.

Wendy is off today, and she can tell something is wrong. "What's going on, Leah? You've seemed so much better the last few days, and suddenly you're right back in a slump. What happened?" She looks concerned.

I tell her about the wire I found in my sandwich yesterday.

Her eyes fly open wide. "Are you serious? Did you call the police?"

I sigh. "No. I don't know what they would have done about it. Probably tell me that I put it there myself for attention."

I'm annoyed at myself and scared of the whole situation. "The doctor said post-concussion symptoms could make me extra emotional, possibly even paranoid." Can I even trust myself now?

I flop back onto the couch, exhausted even though I just woke up. "I don't know how much worse this can get."

"Leah, someone must have done this on purpose." Wendy wants answers.

I get it, I do. But how much of this is in my head? I shrug. "I can't imagine who would want to hurt me."

We're both silent for a moment.

"Are you going to be okay?" Wendy finally asks.

"I honestly don't know," I tell her. "I actually called Nan yesterday, and I feel worse than if I hadn't."

Wendy looks at me sympathetically. "I'm so sorry, Leah. Do you miss home?"

"Every day. But I can't ever go back. Too much has happened."

Wendy looks sad. "You don't think enough time has passed?" She sits next to me on the couch and holds my hand, comforting me.

"No. I really don't know if there will be a passage of time that makes everything okay again. I feel like I'm lost in an eternal loop of misery."

There is really nothing I can do right now to make everything okay. I keep getting this feeling in my stomach like something has to give.

But I'm afraid of what that something is.

A while later, I head over to Sanderson's to teach Bill how to use the page I set up for him. I have him get the laptop from his apartment upstairs. It will be easier to show him on the computer, and we can work on the phone another time.

Bill is absolutely enthralled with everything we can do online. It's like he just found out another universe exists.

In addition to showing him how to run the social media page, we find a new supplier for some of his stock at 20% less than he's paying now.

As we're browsing, an ad pops up. *Meet singles in your area now!* Bill looks startled and intrigued.

I laugh and tell him if he's interested in that, I will guide him to a reputable site, but not to click on any pop-ups.

He blushes and closes the ad, mumbling about how he's not ready for that yet.

I end up staying for three hours, but by the end, Bill can make a new post, answer a message and upload pictures correctly. It's a good afternoon, and I'm glad that I took the time to create the page.

I say goodbye to Bill and tell him that we'll keep working on it. He'll be an internet whiz in no time.

He's engrossed in reading the social media pages of the other businesses in Ashbourne, looking for ways to be more like them. He's a good student.

On my way out the door, I'm stopped by a group of women in their mid-to-late twenties. They've heard about my "miracle cures," and each of them is looking for me to make something to help their various problems: headaches, cracked heels, dry eyes and even a nose rinse.

I let them all know that treatments for these things can be bought over the counter at any pharmacy, but they're explicitly looking for more holistic remedies. I take their numbers and agree to help them.

It's incredible that even as my life is falling apart, this town seems to have made plans for me. I don't know if agreeing to help is the right thing, but it keeps me occupied, and if it helps someone, then all the better.

The group of women thanks me and then walks away, chattering with excitement.

As I walk out to my car, the hair on the back of my neck stands up. I turn around, and Carla is staring at me from about 20 feet away, right outside Sanderson's.

She shakes her head at me, slowly, to show her complete disappointment that I'm still making remedies. As I back up a few steps and turn around toward my car, Lilly steps in front of me from between two parked SUVs.

She looks annoyed. Her cherubic face is red, and she points a finger and pokes me in the chest.

I stumble backward from the shock.

"My mom says you shouldn't be doing that!" she whispers at me. She takes a step forward and tries to poke me again, but I sidestep her, rush to my car and lock the door behind me.

Lilly walks over to the driver's door and peers in the window. "Stop making my mom mad!" She raises her voice to be heard through the closed window.

I put the car in reverse and drive away as fast as I can, my heart thumping in my chest and my palms slick with sweat.

Is this harassment?

Should I call the police?

Tell them what... a child spoke to me harshly?

I press my tongue to the roof of my mouth. It's still sore even if the hole is nearly closed.

I drive home in a daze.

I can feel myself unraveling again, and I'm not sure how to reel it all back in.

For a time, being at Wendy's, things felt like they were getting better, but they're not. They're only getting worse.

It might be time to make a phone call, but I'm going to sleep on it.

Wendy is still at home when I arrive, and I tell her what happened today outside Sanderson's with Carla and Lilly.

She can't believe it. "How could Carla start to drag her little girl into this? She's coming unraveled over homeopathic remedies. It doesn't make any sense; you're making products I would sell at my own store. They're far less likely to hurt people than drugs could." She shakes her head, trying to process what I've told her.

"I honestly don't know. I'm triggering her, but I don't understand how." I'm lying on the couch with an ice pack on my forehead. My headache has been worse again for the last two days. Whether it's from stress or the concussion is hard to guess.

"We have to do something about this, Leah. This can't keep happening. Something has to change. Maybe I should talk to her? She likes me. I could talk some sense into her?" Wendy sounds hopeful.

"I really don't think so. Whatever she has against me has turned personal, whether I like it or not. I miss the days when she only annoyed me with endless conversation at the store."

Wendy sighs. "We have to do something," she repeats, as if saying it again will give us a better idea.

I tell her I'm going to make dinner, and we can brainstorm while we eat.

In the kitchen, it feels good to focus on measuring, stirring, sautéing and broiling. It helps to have other tasks to fixate on besides Carla and my life, which is essentially in shambles.

I set the table with nice plates and flatware. We're being fancy tonight. I even light some pillar candles like we're having a dinner party for two.

We eat roast chicken, potatoes, green beans and a peach galette for dessert.

The normalcy makes me feel slightly better.

Wendy has a glass of wine, but I abstain because it doesn't feel right yet, still healing from the concussion.

After dinner, we share dish duty and then curl up on the couch to watch something lighthearted to help us relax before bed.

Once we start yawning, we know it's time to turn in.

I go to take Maisie out for one last pee and realize we didn't put out the dinner candles. They've burned down to almost nubs.

I blow them out, and the smoky scent fills the kitchen for a moment. It's gone by the time we're back inside.

Maisie and I curl up in what is feeling less like the guest bedroom and more like "our" bedroom every day. I fall asleep stroking her fur to the sounds of her comforting snores.

Thirty-Four

My ears are ringing.
Why is it so bright?
Am I still in the ER?
No, that noise is real.
What is it?
I sit up in bed.
Maisie is already up, every hackle on her body raised. A deep growl escapes her. It's a sound I've never heard her make before.
I smell smoke.
The fire alarm is going off.
I look out the window and see orange flames licking at the side of the house. I jump out of bed, grab Maisie and stumble to the door.
There's a distinct crackling sound as the fire licks at and then consumes the window casing.
The room has started to fill with smoke, and as I open the bedroom door, it billows out into the hallway. Running out into the living room, I see Wendy emerging, half-asleep, from her bedroom.
"Is there a fire?" she yells to me.
I can taste the smoke.
"Yes! We have to get out!"
We crawl through the living room and out into the main foyer, grasping for the doorknob.
The door opens, and we spill out onto her lawn. It took less than a minute to get out, but it feels like it's happened in slow motion.
We clutch each other, terrified, watching the right side of the house being engulfed in flames.
Neither of us grabbed our phones on the way out.

Wendy runs for the neighbor's house in her pajamas, barefoot, to call 911.

Nothing makes sense. It's as if the world around me is background noise.

I hear Wendy as she comes back, saying the fire department is on the way.

A group of neighbors has gathered on Wendy's lawn. One has brought blankets, and another brings us slippers so we don't freeze while we wait for the firefighters.

I stare at the blaze, entranced.

I notice the cameras on the side of her house have melted. I doubt any footage that may have been helpful is still recoverable.

Wendy stands next to me. She's holding my hand.

The fire truck pulls up, along with an ambulance. The EMTs take us for a checkup to make sure we haven't inhaled too much smoke. The firefighters are now dousing the house in water, trying to quell the flames.

It looks like it's spreading more than it's being put out.

The EMTs ask for my name and if I was inside when the fire started. They check my nose and throat, my breathing. They hook me up to machines to test my oxygen and carbon monoxide levels.

It all feels like it's happening to someone else.

The police are next. I want to ask them if this happened because I *forgot to close the door*, but I don't. They ask basic questions of both Wendy and me.

"Are you both residents? Both homeowners?"

"Could there be others inside? Pets?"

"Whose bedroom is on the right side?"

After they finish their initial questions, they tell us to check back in with the paramedics to make sure we're okay.

We sit on the back of the ambulance in silence, watching as the firefighters continue to save what's left of Wendy's house.

Most of the home's right side has been reduced to smoldering embers. Her garage, my temporary bedroom and part of the kitchen no longer exist except for ash.

Wendy reaches for my hand and squeezes.

She didn't deserve this.

This happened because of me.

I've ruined her life as well as my own.

She squeezes my hand as if she knows it now, too.

I should be panicked, but I'm numb again.

I continue watching as a few embers from the fire have caught the wind. They dance wildly through the sky and then land, burning the grass just under our feet.

I do have to make that phone call today.

"You okay?" Wendy sounds slightly hoarse. I can't tell if it's from the smoke or from emotion, but it's probably both.

"No," I say honestly. "I'm not okay. My life is a wreck, and now I've dragged you down with me. I can't stay in Ashbourne anymore. I'm going to have to leave."

In true Wendy fashion, she attempts to make me feel better, despite us sitting in front of her home, now half-rubble. "Leah, you can't go..."

"Sorry to interrupt, ladies, but there's a federal task force here, and they need to speak with you." The officer is looking at me while he says it.

Wendy looks shocked. "What would the Feds be doing here? How is this even on their radar?"

We climb down off the back of the ambulance and are escorted past a large van with no markings.

I start to sweat. This van looks an awful lot like the one I was abducted in.

The officer leads us to a small tactical area set up with space heaters, chairs and computers. We sit, thankful to be near warmth for a moment.

"What is going on?" Wendy is confused.

I don't blame her.

But I can't bring myself to say it out loud.

The van doors open, and light spills onto the black pavement of the street. A tall, dark-haired woman in uniform steps out, carrying a laptop. She flashes her badge at us.

"Deputy U.S. Marshal Elizabeth Pratt, I'm with Witness Security."

"Witness Security?" Wendy is now doubly confused. "I don't understand."

The Marshal gives Wendy a look. "Your friend does."

I'm sweating from head to toe.

"Right, Della?"

Thirty-Five

"Who is Della?" Wendy is now completely bewildered.

She looks at me, and I can see her starting to put the pieces together. Constantly worried about being seen. Paying cash whenever possible. Needing to leave my entire life in California. Recurring issues and escalating tension with someone in town.

Now, federal witness protection is here.

Deputy Pratt gives me a hard look. "Sorry, Della. We don't have the luxury of secrecy now."

Wendy is incredulous. "Leah?" She looks as though I just slapped her.

I start to apologize. "Wendy, I—"

"Excuse me, ladies," the Marshal interrupts. "We have some footage to share with you. Your cameras melted in the fire, but the video is stored in the cloud. We subpoenaed it, and I think you'll be interested in what it shows."

She puts the laptop on the table and turns it around so we can see, then presses play.

It's five seconds of Wendy's driveway on a November night, and then we see her.

Carla is running full speed toward the house with her clothes billowing behind her.

Fifteen seconds later, you can see the smoke begin to rise in front of the camera. It blocks part of the recording, but you can just make out Carla's shape walking away from the flames.

Wendy and I look at each other in horror.

"I... I can't believe she would do this," I hear myself say. "I knew she didn't like me and was getting increasingly more agitated, but I didn't think she would actually try to harm me. Us."

Wendy is also in disbelief. "Why? Why would she do this?"

The Marshal interrupts us again, seemingly not caring much for the "why."

"We have Carla in custody. She turned herself in and has confessed to lighting the fire." She turns to Wendy. "I'm sorry for the loss of your home. Aggravated arson is a felony, and with a full confession, Carla is going to be facing years, if not decades, behind bars."

Wendy gasps, trying to process everything that is happening right now.

I sigh, glad that Carla is no longer a threat, but even more worried that I hadn't thought she was.

"What happens now?" I ask the Marshal.

"For tonight, the two of you will go to a hotel a few towns away. Try to rest and get some sleep. We're going to need you tomorrow and over the next few days to take statements, but you're still in shock and need to rest before we can do that."

With that, she gets up, and another officer comes to collect us. We're led to an unmarked black sedan, and both get in the back, Maisie sitting between us. She sees we won't be opening a window, so she lies down with her head in my lap.

Wendy and I say very little as we're transported to the hotel. There's so much to say, and I'm not sure where to start.

Wendy stares out the window and doesn't try to engage. The moon illuminates her face, casting shadows that make her look almost angry.

Or maybe she is angry. She has every right to be.

We pull up to the hotel and are brought directly to a room on the 5th floor. The officer with us says there will be a guard on standby outside the door all night, and that if we need anything, we should let them know.

Where would we even start?

The room has two double beds, each with a small box full of clothes, shoes and toiletries. I sit on one bed, while Maisie jumps up and lies at the foot. Wendy sits on the edge of the other. She lies down, staring at the ceiling. Her face is streaked with soot and tears. The smell of smoke clings to everything—our pajamas, skin and hair.

"Wendy?" I say, tentatively. I can't read her right now. She looks lost.

"I don't know what to say right now, Leah. I mean, Della? Whoever you really are."

She sits back up, and her face is heartbreakingly sad. Her eyes fill with tears again. "Why did you think you couldn't trust me with the truth? I've always been there for you. Have I ever given you reason to think I wouldn't be?" She's wringing her hands now, as the tears start to fall again. "I don't know what to believe anymore. How much of what you've told me is even the truth?"

"Wendy, I'm so sorry. I never meant to get you wrapped up in all of this. I tried so hard to deal with my issues on my own for such a long time. I cut myself off from the world. You are the only real friend I've had in nearly three years."

My own tears fall now, too. "Everything I've ever told you was the truth. Well, except my name, of course. The rest is true; it's just not everything."

A strand of hair falls in my face, and it smells like smoke, and weirdly, like cinnamon.

Wendy looks small and hurt, sitting on the hotel bed with her shoulders slumped.

I don't blame her.

"My real name is Della Russo. I truly was a top scientist at ChemGen. Everything I told you about the clinical trial was real, and it did end my career."

I take a deep breath as I prepare to tell her the rest, which connects so many dots of my spotty past. "What you *don't* know is that when the board pressed me to approve the clinical trial, they didn't only want the drug tested on adults, they also wanted the drug approved for ages five and up, as soon as physically possible. It's the biggest reason I was so skeptical about moving to trials so fast, even though the data looked good."

Wendy's face changes for a minute, but her arms are still crossed over her chest.

I pause a moment and try to breathe through the panic that is rising in me, despite knowing that there is almost nothing left to lose.

Well, nothing besides Wendy, anyway.

"When the clinical trial went sideways, more than half of the participants were injured in some way. Some were harmed irreparably, and others were luckier and only sustained milder drug-related injuries."

I pause, not wanting to go on, but I do. "I brought these findings to the board, certain that they would shut it down. But for reasons I can't explain, they didn't want to." I let my own confusion bleed through this explanation. I still don't understand why this happened. It never made sense to me.

Wendy's face still looks angry, but she doesn't stop me, so I continue. "At that point, I made a choice, and this time I was determined to make the correct one. I stayed, promising to set up another clinical trial, but instead I gathered paperwork and went to the police. I blew the whistle on ChemGen." I've been staring at the floor as I recount the rest of my story, but I peek up, afraid of how Wendy is taking this news.

Wendy is now staring at me in a state of disbelief. "You gave up everything to make sure nobody else would get hurt," she says softly.

I wish that were the case. "That's not entirely true. I had no idea that things would go as wrong as they have. I was fired, and the trial dragged on for months, actually close to a year."

Breathe, Della, breathe.

"Before I was set to testify, I had the kidnapping scare while running in the park. All of that is true. But it happened because the rich men on the board were trying to silence me, keep the truth from getting out. I'm sure they wanted me to disappear forever." I look up, and Wendy is leaning forward, enthralled with my story.

I continue. "I was put into a safe house and guarded until the trial was over. ChemGen was found guilty of multiple counts of fraud, criminal negligence and violations of FDA regulations.

"At that point, I thought I would be able to go back to something resembling a normal life, even though my career was over. Who was going to hire a scientist who outed her prior company?"

Wendy is still watching me, transfixed. She gets up and moves next to me. She picks up my hand tentatively to hold it as I finish trying to explain.

"It somehow got worse. A few of the board members just... disappeared. Probably to somewhere in Mexico or South America, maybe Europe. With the prior attempt on my life, the federal prosecutor recommended that I go into witness protection until they could be apprehended."

I'm crying now, and I don't try to stop the well of tears. "In the years since, all but one have been apprehended: Vance Calder. The rest were overconfident that their money could keep them safe, and they didn't try to become invisible."

I put my head in my hands, trying not to sob as I tell Wendy the whole story. "Vance was always the one I was least afraid of. He was a family man who seemed to be in the business for the right reasons. But he's still out there, and you never know. I mean, I can't be sure."

I look up at her again. "It's been over two years since the trial ended, and I became 'Leah.' All this time, I've been hoping that this nightmare would eventually end and I could go home. It's why I've shut people out for my entire life in Ashbourne. I don't know who, if anyone, I can trust."

I look at Wendy. "Except you. You're the only person here I know I can trust, and I'm so sorry that I didn't tell you everything. I brought you into so much danger because I didn't want to believe that I could be found after all this time. I needed you to ground me, to keep myself sane. And it was selfish of me. I don't blame you if you can never forgive me." I put my head back in my hands, wishing yet again that I was someone else, in a different time and place.

"Le... Della," she says, as if she's saying a word in a language she doesn't speak. "I wish you had told me earlier, but I understand why you couldn't. I can't imagine what you've been through, what it must be like to live every day in that kind of fear." She looks at me, almost tenderly. "I'll get used to your name. It may be weird for a while, but we can get through this together."

I smile sadly. "Call me Ellie."

She hugs me, and for a moment, we're both crying.

When we finally let go of each other, Wendy has a thoughtful look on her face. "Something I don't understand at all. What does Carla have to do with any of this?"

I sigh. "I truly, honestly have no idea. I don't know if her escalations are related to my past, just that they've dragged everything out into the open. They've made me visible in a way that isn't safe for me."

There's a quiet knock at the door, and Wendy and I look at each other. I get up and look through the peephole into the hallway.

Mina is at the door.

Thirty-Six

I turn around and look at Wendy, confused. "It's Mina."

"What?" she asks, as if she thinks she didn't quite hear me right.

I open the door slowly. Mina is standing there, next to the agent guarding our room. He allowed Mina to come up and knock.

Should I let her in? "Um, hi?" I say. I'm not sure if it's a question or a statement.

"Hi, Leah," she says. "Can I come in?"

I look to the agent posted outside the door. He doesn't look back at me. "Uh, okay," I say, opening the door wide enough for her to slip through, and then closing and locking it behind her.

She steps inside and realizes Wendy is also in the room. "Oh, hi, Wendy. I wasn't told you were here, too." For a minute, she looks lost, like she isn't sure what to say next.

She *wasn't told?* Who told her *I* was here?

"Um, Leah, would I be able to talk to you in private for a few moments?"

I don't understand what she's doing here, or how our guard let her through without issue, but I'm not going anywhere with her alone.

"I think I'm more comfortable here, with Wendy," I say.

With everything that has happened, I don't trust anyone right now.

"Alright," Mina says, "but what I have to discuss with you is related to, well, federal matters."

I look at Mina, in shock, trying to process what she just told me. "Mina, are you with witness protection?"

Has she really pretended to be my friend for the last few weeks? How much of what she's told me about herself is true?

Wow. I sound like a hypocrite right now.

Mina looks at Wendy as if she is uncomfortable, then back at me. "Wendy?" she asks.

"Wendy knows now," I tell her, sitting back on the bed and smoothing out the comforter. "Kind of unfair to leave her in the dark when we were brought to a hotel under federal protection because it's my fault her house burned down."

Mina nods, more settled now that she knows how much Wendy understands. "Yes, Lea... Della, I'm a Deputy Marshal assigned to the witness protection unit. My branch likes to settle people in or near the hometowns of agents, so that we can keep tabs without being suspicious."

She looks at me and can read the sadness on my face. "Please don't be upset. Everything we've shared is real. I've been doing my job, trying to make sure you didn't get hurt. But the friendship we've built is genuine."

"Maybe you're not very good at your job, then," I say angrily.

I'm hurt that I didn't see through her, that I trusted her, allowed her to get close to me in ways that nobody but Wendy has in years, and that I was so insanely wrong.

I cross my arms over my chest, wishing she would go away.

Mina flinches but absorbs the angry words as if she deserves them. "You're right, Della. Carla wasn't even on my radar. We had no idea that she planned to harm you."

I don't meet her eyes.

I can hear the discomfort in her voice as she tries to do her job. "Do you have any idea what set her off? Caused her to escalate the way she has?"

"Mina, I don't know if I can talk to you right now."

I'm reeling from this newest revelation. My life these days is like trying to stay upright while standing in the middle of an earthquake.

Shockingly, Wendy answers her. "Leah, I mean... Ellie and I believe Carla has been escalating because Ellie has been more visible in the community lately, making holistic remedies for folks around town.

"She's been using her scientific knowledge and her background in holistic medicine to help people. It's the only thing we can think of that has really changed." Wendy looks to Mina to see how much of this information translates.

Mina runs her fingers through her hair, processing what Wendy's told her. As she's thinking, running logistics in her head, Wendy speaks again.

"What does Carla have to do with Ellie's past?" She seems determined to find answers that, right now, I don't have the emotional aptitude to process.

Mina's face softens, and it takes her a moment to answer. "When we questioned Carla tonight, we found that Lilly was one of the children who was injured in the failed ChemGen trial."

The room is silent for a moment, but tears run down my and Wendy's faces. The cinnamon smell is stronger than it's been in weeks.

She waits a moment for us to absorb this information before continuing. "She moved here shortly after you were placed, Della. Like I said before, she wasn't even on our radar. She seemed harmless." Mina stops for a moment, and her breath catches.

"Questioning her tonight, we learned she's just a mom who was heartbroken because of what happened to her child. It was like she wanted to keep you close so she would have an outlet for her grief."

I suddenly realize why Mina seemed familiar to me on the first night I met her. It's because she's been part of my life, though I didn't know it, for years. She's been popping in and out of Ashbourne for two years to keep an eye on me.

Wendy is beside herself. What we've learned is tragic in a way that's difficult to comprehend. Lilly's issues are a direct result of my negligence. Her limp and advanced asthma are entirely my fault.

No wonder Carla hates me; she has every right to.

"I'm sorry to have to be the one to tell you all this, but I felt like I owed it to you on a personal level. I know you're angry, and you have every right to be, but I wasn't 'pretending' to be your friend. We really did connect in a way that I haven't felt in Ashbourne, maybe ever." Mina blushes and looks at the floor.

Even in my state of shock and exhaustion, I can see that what she did is really no different than what I did to Wendy.

If I'm being honest with myself, what she did is *better* than what I did to Wendy. I was dragging my friend down with me. Mina was trying to shield me, whether it was her job or not.

"I'm going to take a shower and try to wash tonight, hell, the past two weeks, off me," Wendy says, grabbing the ill-fitting clothes out of her box. I think it's probably to give Mina and me some privacy, but she plays it off well.

Wendy slips off to the bathroom, and I hear the shower start running.

Mina is still standing near the doorway. She looks uncomfortable, like she doesn't know whether she should leave or not.

I sigh. "Mina, please come sit down."

She looks at me, seemingly grateful to know that wherever we stand, she's still welcome in my space.

There aren't any chairs in the room, so she sits on Wendy's bed, looking uneasy. I think she doesn't want to assume it's okay with Wendy.

"It's fine," I sigh, letting my anger with her go. "Sit here." I point to a spot next to me on the bed.

She looks surprised but relieved not to be sitting where she isn't sure she's welcome. She sits down, rubbing the back of her neck with a hand as if all the stress of the last few weeks has settled there. "Leah," she starts. Then she looks at me. "I mean, Della..."

"It's okay." I smile sadly at her. "You can call me Ellie."

Thirty-Seven

"Oh... okay, Ellie," Mina begins. "I... I don't know how to tell you how sorry I am for all of this. I never meant for things to get personal, but sometimes it's hard to separate the job from the person."

Her voice catches in her throat. "Especially in this case. I was trying to protect you, to do my job, but I let my guard down. I let you down, both as a Marshal and as your friend. I don't know how or if I can make things right." Her eyes are slightly misty, and I'm taken aback because Mina is always so measured and calm.

I want to be angry at her. Lashing out would be easier. I could push her away, and we could never speak again.

But deep down, I know that's not what I want. The part of me that trusted Mina when I knew I shouldn't trust anyone was still right. She never set out to harm me. Sure, she ended up bruising my ego, but that's a small price to pay for a true friend.

I slide my hand across the bed so that our pinkies are touching. "Thank you, Mina. I'm sorry for what I said earlier. It's been such a shocking few days. A few weeks, really, but the last few days have really been awful. I understand, I really do. It's no different than me keeping my past from Wendy."

Mina looks at me, relieved that everything is out in the open now.

I'm relieved, too. I know I'm at greater risk of exposure now, especially with the fire, but if WITSEC can keep my name and picture out of the local papers, I may be able to stay here.

She smiles at me, a small, nervous smile and for a minute, I think of the shy, lanky kid she was growing up, and my heart hurts for her.

"Do you know if you'll get to stay on my case, or if you'll be reassigned?" I ask. I want her to stay. In ways I don't quite understand, I need her to stay.

"I'm not sure what will happen, but for now, you're safe."

My eyes fill, but the tears don't fall yet.

"Don't worry, Ellie, it's going to be okay." Mina scoots closer to me on the bed and puts an arm around me. I lean into her, and the tears come.

"Is it?" I ask, suddenly angry. "I trust you. I know you're here. If they reassign you, it means someone else will be watching me. I'll be looking over my shoulder again constantly. For the rest of my life, I won't know who I can trust." I bury my head in her shoulder and realize how melodramatic that sounded, like a child being told she can't have another cookie.

Mina brushes a strand of hair from my face and says in a soft voice, "I'm not going anywhere."

I sit up, watching her closely. "What? What does that mean?"

She sighs and crosses her legs on the bed, facing me now. "I'm tired, Ellie. I'm tired of the stress of my job. I'm not 25 anymore, and everything seems to keep piling up.

"I've spent decades running from my past. Even if they don't reassign me, I'm thinking of stepping down. You've taught me a lot in the last few weeks, even if you don't know it."

I look at her, dumbfounded. How on earth have I taught her anything?

She continues. "I know that I said I have a great life where I live now, but if I'm honest with myself, with you, it's pretty lonely. My parents are getting older, and they need more help than ever. My history is here, in Ashbourne. Maybe my future is, too." She looks away as she says it, like she's ashamed to have this full-circle realization in front of someone, and not privately.

"I think that's amazing, Mina. If that's what feels right to you, I think you should pursue it." I give her a genuine smile. I'm so glad that we both opened up here tonight. Maybe just as my life is falling apart, it's being put back together in a way that I can live with.

Thirty-Eight

The next few days are busy. We give our statements multiple times and live out of the hotel, eating fast food.

Mina visits daily to make sure we're okay, bringing us new clothes, better toiletries and restaurant takeout.

She apologizes for not knowing how to cook, but we laugh and are grateful to have something other than greasy burgers to eat.

On our last day in the hotel, there's a knock on the door. I look through the peephole and smile.

It's Mina.

"Hey!" she greets me. She's carrying a Greek takeout bag, and I'm irrationally excited.

"Greek takeout? Tell me you got falafel!" My mouth is already watering.

She smiles. "Um, of course I did."

Wendy and I attack the bag, and for a moment, Mina looks taken aback.

Then she laughs as we settle in to eat.

"So," Mina begins in a more serious voice than normal, "I have some news."

Wendy and I look up from our feast, mouths full. "What's up?"

Mina sighs. "Well, we searched Carla's house yesterday. What we found was disturbing, to say the least."

I stop chewing. Now she's got my attention. "Okay. Seriously, what?"

Mina runs her fingers through her hair. I've come to realize this is how she copes when she's nervous. "We found journals, photographs, paintings, et cetera. She wasn't just casually watching; she was actively stalking you." She shivers and looks at the floor. "I don't know how I missed it. It was right under my nose."

"Mina." I'm floored. "It's not your fault. Nobody thought she was a real threat. Even me, and I suspect everyone."

"I know, but it was my job to protect you. And I failed spectacularly. I was looking for corporate goons or hired assassins, not traumatized moms." Sitting on the bed, she puts her head in her hands. "We never clocked her as dangerous; there were no red flags."

A question pops into my head. "How did she find me?"

Mina shakes her head. "We're still not entirely sure. What we do know is that for about 18 months following Lilly's... um... accident, they lived roughly 20 minutes from here in Havenfield. They moved to Ashbourne just a few months after you moved."

She sighs, frustrated. "Our best guess is that she happened to see you somewhere and everything clicked into place. Since then, she's been doing her best to irritate you in any way she could."

I think back to when I first moved here. I don't remember much, though I did visit Havenfield a few times. There's a Walmart there.

Wendy chimes in. "So, what was in the journals?"

"Everything, pretty much. Little things, like 'accidentally' spilling hot coffee on you, letting the air out of your tires, breaking in to light a candle and then putting it back out. She would take your laundry but then bring it back. It seems like everything she did was more to ruin your day than to hurt you."

Now, I'm stunned. "She broke in? How?"

"Well, not exactly 'broke in.' Somehow, she had a copy of your key. One of the journals outlines how hard it was to get it, then get back to you without you noticing. That's what happened the night of the 'break-in'. She didn't even go inside, just unlocked it and left it open to freak you out."

My stomach drops. This whole time, I wasn't crazy. She was trying to ruin my life in a million tiny ways.

"What about the fire? And the shelf?"

Mina shakes her head. "That's the weirdest part—no mention of either. The best I can come up with is that the shelf was truly an accident, and the fire wasn't planned. Then it happened so fast she didn't have time to write it down."

I know I look alarmed because Mina adds quickly, "It's okay. She confessed. She's going to prison for a long time."

I relax slightly. The nightmare is over.

Then I think of something else. "What will happen to Lilly?" The thought of her being ripped from her mom makes me sad, regardless of what Carla did.

Mina looks sad, too. "She has an aunt in upstate New York who she's going to live with. From what I hear, they're well off and have other kids her age. The agent who spoke to her said they're going to look into intensive physical therapy for Lilly's leg and the best pulmonologist in New York for her asthma. It sounds like her life is going to be better than it was, spent with a mom hell-bent on revenge."

"Yeah," I say softly. I can't imagine that's a great environment to grow up in, but I can't imagine losing your mom for the rest of your childhood, either.

I put down my falafel.

I'm suddenly not hungry anymore.

Thirty-Nine

Once WITSEC has confirmed that the imminent danger is over, we house-hunt for a rental while Wendy's is being rebuilt. We find one that's fully furnished just after Thanksgiving.

By Christmas, we're planning a grand dinner with Mina and Bill.

Wendy and I make turkey, stuffing, homemade cranberry sauce, mashed potatoes, green bean casserole and multiple pies.

Wendy accidentally burns one, and the acrid, smoky smell fills the small kitchen. I open a window to let it out, waving the smoke outside with a potholder.

Bill arrives first, bringing produce from the store to make a basic salad. He hands me the bag and says, "Thanks for inviting me."

I smile at him fondly. "Thanks for coming, Bill. I'm glad you're here."

Bill still calls me "Leah," but is adjusting to Wendy and Mina calling me "Ellie," even though he doesn't understand it.

The three of us agreed to keep my background quiet from everyone else. It's not something that matters in the scheme of things, and the more people who know, the riskier it is for me to stay here.

Mina rings the bell next. "Merry Christmas!" she says, handing me two bottles of wine.

I'm glad she didn't cook; wine is much better than her attempts.

We sit down to eat, and Wendy raises her glass in a toast. "To old friendships, and new beginnings!" She smiles broadly at her friends around the table, and we all dig in.

"So, Bill," Wendy says with a mouth full of turkey. "Seems like business is booming lately. What are you doing differently?" She is always looking to pick people's brains for ways to make Root more visible to the public.

Bill pulls out his phone. "Well, Leah showed me how to use social media, so I've been making advertisements daily, posting about specials, and my newest thing is creating funny reels to make people laugh."

He looks a little perplexed as he adds, "I think people come in to visit me as much as they do for goods."

He pulls up a reel of himself, critiquing his own painting. It's the one of the dog filling the gas tank. "*And as you can see, I stink at painting!*" He looks to the camera with a wide grin, while a laugh track plays behind him.

"The darndest thing is, people have started coming in and buying my terrible paintings. It's like it's a souvenir from the store." He shakes his head as if he doesn't understand, but he's smiling.

He isn't quite sure what he's doing right, but he knows it's working.

I put down my fork and look at him seriously. "I hear that you may have gained a new friend with your reels, Bill." I let a small smile creep onto my face. I can't help teasing him; it's so easy.

"Leah!" he says, blushing. He shifts uneasily in his chair and runs his hand over the top of his head. "It's exactly that, she's a *friend*. Nothing more. We've been talking through online chat. I haven't even met her in real life."

The rest of us laugh, and the red in Bill's cheeks deepens. I didn't even think that was possible.

"Bill," I say, still laughing, "we're happy for you. Even if she's just a friend, I'm so glad you met someone you can connect with." I look at him fondly and reach across the table to grab his hand. "Honestly, don't be embarrassed. It's great."

Bill smiles and squeezes my hand. "Thanks, Leah." He looks genuinely happy.

I turn to Mina. "How is the job search going? Any leads?"

Her mouth is full of potatoes, and she holds up a finger to give herself a minute to chew.

"It's actually going really well," she says once she's washed her potatoes down with some wine. "I've gotten lots of interview requests, and many of them are remote work. It needs to either be remote or local to be worth it. But honestly, it's been nice to be 'retired'." She kicks back in her chair, looking relaxed.

Mina asks, "Wendy, how is the rebuild going?" The two of them have grown more comfortable since the fire. It feels like Mina is finally learning to put the past behind her.

"Oh, God," Wendy says, laughing. "It's a nightmare. But, upside, I get the kitchen remodel I've been planning for the last two years!" She's finished her meal and is starting to clear the plates from the table.

I get up to help her. We load the dishwasher together so that the majority of the mess is cleaned while we eat dessert. Once that is taken care of, we bring the pies to the table.

Except for the one Wendy burned; that one went in the trash.

It's a good thing that we made two pumpkin pies.

As we set them down, Bill and Mina groan that they're too full to eat dessert yet.

"No rush," I tell them. "It's here when you're ready."

We take our wine and go into the living room to relax.

Everyone is quiet for a few minutes.

Bill is texting, probably with his new friend.

He was shocked to find out what Carla had done. Like the rest of us, he never thought that she would turn violent. He's in the dark about her motives, but he's written it off as craziness on her part.

Wendy and I are still processing what we've been through. It's been about a month and a half, and the newfound peace has been welcome—no more notes, voicemails, break-ins or anything else "unlucky" that keeps me looking over my shoulder.

The unease I used to feel has nearly evaporated. Having two friends who know my whole story has changed everything.

There isn't a greater gift than this.

We hang out until we've got room for pie.

I have two pieces.

When dessert and coffee are finished, Bill says he has gifts for us.

We unwrap the poorly packaged presents, and they're his paintings from the store. He wanted us to always have a piece of him in our homes.

I got "bats and the moon."

I love it.

When Wendy's place is rebuilt, I'll hang it in my room.

Bill says he has to go; there are lots of plans to make for tomorrow's after-Christmas sale.

"Thank you all," he says sincerely. "It's nice to have friends to spend the holidays with."

I tell him to wait and make him a plate of leftovers to take home for later.

"Drive safe!" I yell out the door as he gets into his truck.

There's a perfectly cozy amount of "Christmas snow" outside, and while the roads aren't bad, I told him to text me when he gets home.

I start back to the living room but pause outside.

Mina and Wendy are talking softly, almost like they don't want me to hear it.

"I just... I'm so sorry, Mina. For everything when we were kids. I had no idea how much it affected you, how much it would have mattered if I had spoken up, said *something*. If I had even reached out and been nice, instead of pretending like the bullying didn't exist." Her voice catches in her throat, and I imagine there are probably tears in her eyes.

Mina interrupts her. "It's okay, Wendy, really. Yeah, it hurt as a kid, but the last few months, more than ever, have taught me that letting go of the past is the best thing we can do for ourselves. Wendy, don't cry, it's really okay." I can hear the concern in Mina's voice.

"No, I need to get this off my chest. It's something you've deserved from me for years. Ellie called me out on it shortly before the fire, and it messed with my mind for a while. It was like she was referencing a version of me that I didn't remember, that I didn't even think existed. But the more I thought about it, the more I realized she was right. I've been replaying scenes from when we were kids in my head, over and over. I know it's true. I wasn't one of the bullies, but I wasn't kind either. And not being "unkind" isn't an excuse. I'm so sorry, Mina. I know you forgive me, but I wanted you to know how I feel." Wendy is sniffling. Now I'm sure she's crying.

"Thank you. That means more to me than you could know. And honestly? I'd rather have a good relationship now than have had one when we were kids. You're a good person, Wendy. I'm proud to call you my friend."

Listening to my two best friends heal a decades-old divide is also healing something within me.

I peek through the doorway, and the two of them are hugging it out.

I couldn't be happier. The two people I would trust with my life are now true friends.

Two minutes later, I come through the door carrying a wine bottle. "Okay, who needs more wine?"

Forty

I've really been leaning into homemade remedies lately. I invested in some mixing tools, vials and a variety of pots and jars. I'm taking local requests but also creating things I think are universal, like sleeping tinctures or tea for a stuffy nose. I'm working on a name for my product line, and Wendy has already said that when I'm ready, she'll have a shelf at Root waiting for me.

I still work at Sanderson's, but I think if my hobby takes off enough, I may cut back to part-time.

I won't quit; I like working with Bill, especially now that he spends more time out front asking what I think of his newest marketing endeavor or taking videos to edit for reels.

He's gotten pretty good at video editing. He's a natural.

The store really is booming these days. Tourists come in to take pictures with Bill and buy his paintings, which I would never in a million years have guessed could happen. It's a good thing he has a backstock, because he doesn't paint as much these days.

I'm off today, so I'm spending my morning working on remedies.

I have a few deliveries to make around town, so when I finish up, I grab the packages and get in the car. Maisie comes with me, and I turn up the heat and crack the window for her. Even though it's cold, it's worth seeing her happy.

I won't deliver to people's homes.

Enough of my hesitation around people has carried over that I still try to protect myself in basic common-sense ways. No home deliveries, and I keep pepper spray on my keychain "just in case."

What I'll do is drop off products at places of business or leave them at Root, with the customer's name on them, in a bin that Wendy made for me. She doesn't mind handing them out.

Maisie comes into Root with me to deliver some packages, and we're instantly surrounded by customers fawning over her. She soaks up the attention like I've never petted her in my life, showing them her belly and thriving in the middle of the puppy chaos she's caused.

I leave her to her newfound fame for a moment and take my packages to Wendy at the counter. "You'd think she was a celebrity," I laugh, as I hand her the parcels.

"Well, she is adorable. And it helps that she's so friendly." Wendy takes my product bin out from under the counter and drops the new ones inside. "When are you going to make enough to stock my shelf? I've been saving it for you for weeks now!" She points to a standing shelf at the checkout that she bought that's currently sitting empty.

I smile at her. "I'll get there, I promise! Things have just been busy lately."

She looks at me skeptically. "Busy? You've done more relaxing than being busy the last month." Her face softens. "Not that you don't... we don't deserve to relax for a change. I know you'll get there when you're ready. And that personal requests come first."

"It's been a rough road, for sure. But at least we're on the other side of it now. I'm building a life here I can live with. *Want* to live with."

I still miss my family so much.

And I've thought about calling Nan again; I've even thought about leaving WITSEC completely.

The thought makes my stomach drop, like the peak of a roller coaster, but I've felt more settled in the last couple of months than I ever have. If nobody has found me yet, who says they're still looking? The trial is over, and another company will soon be testing a similar compound.

Is there still any danger?

I don't think a "revenge plot" makes sense now. There doesn't seem to be much, if anything, at stake anymore. I won't rush the decision, but it's worth considering.

Wendy and I chat for a minute about how she's closing tonight.

I tell her I'll wait till she gets home for dinner.

I can always make a late lunch. It's much better living with her and having someone to share meals, laughs, and time with.

I wonder how different my life would have been if I had moved in with her earlier.

We hug goodbye, and I remove Maisie from her crowd of adoring fans.

She isn't happy about leaving when there are so many people willing to pet her, but in the car, I turn up the heat and put the window down enough for her to stick her nose out. It's a good compromise.

I bring Maisie home, then run back out for groceries. It's been a few days since we shopped, so we're running low on staples. I text Mina from the parking lot,

"What are you doing? Want to come by for lunch?"

She responds immediately. *"Yes. See you in 30?"*

"Sounds perfect," I text back.

Mina and I have a relaxed lunch together, chatting about her interviews, my remedies, and our plans for the future. Suddenly, she gives me a look like she wants to say something but doesn't know how.

"What's on your mind?" I reach across the table and put my hand on top of hers.

"It's... it's nothing, really. I just wanted to say thank you." She looks away toward Maisie, who is rolling on the rug, scratching her back.

I've watched Mina over the last couple of months start to really open up. To me, Wendy, the world.

I'm not sure why she's thanking me. "Thank me for what?"

I'm genuinely confused. She's the one who is still protective of me, even though it's not her job anymore.

She looks at me tentatively. "You've taught me a lot, whether you know it or not. You've been through so much, and here you are. Moving on, living your life. It even seems like, as much as you like to pretend you're still miserable, you're happy. It makes me think about my own past and gives me, sort of, a push that I need to move forward." She looks down, blushing.

I smile. I do like to act as if I'm miserable, but I think it's because the thought of being really happy is scary.

If I'm happy, it means I have people and things in my life that could be taken away.

She's right; I do downplay how happy I am. It's a trauma response that I'm still working through.

"Well, you're welcome for being such an inspiration," I say sarcastically. Mina just laughs.

She leaves around five, and I have a few hours to read, watch TV and hang out with Maisie before I expect Wendy back from Root.

At 9:15 p.m., my phone rings. Wendy's calling.

"Hi!" I answer. "I stopped at the store today; you don't need to grab anything on your way home." She's always so on top of everything. Of course she called to check if there's anything we need.

I hear silence for a moment, and then a man's voice that I vaguely recognize, but I can't place it.

"Hi, Della."

My heart jumps in my chest, and the familiar feeling of the world closing in begins.

"Who... who is this? Where's Wendy?" The panic starts to well up. Everything tightens so I can barely breathe.

The line sounds fuzzy, like he's calling from far away.

"I'm going to give you an address, and you're going to meet us. If you don't, Wendy is going to have a really bad night." I can hear his shallow breathing on the other end of the line.

"How do I know you have her?" With technology these days, maybe he hijacked her number, and he's actually somewhere far away. Wendy could still be closing up at Root, blissfully unaware that this man is using her number to get me somewhere alone.

There's noise on the line, like the phone being moved around clumsily.

Then I hear her.

"Ellie?" The voice sounds scared.

It's Wendy.

"Wendy? Oh my God, where are you? What's going on?" I'm frantic now. I know what's happening, but I don't want to believe it.

The phone is taken from her, and I hear his voice again.

"Write this down, Della, and make sure you get it right. 105 Archer Road, Larkhill. There's an entrance on the left side. Be there in 30 minutes. And if you call the police or text anyone, she's dead. Believe me, I'll know if you do."

He hangs up before I can say another word.

I know exactly who he is.

It's Vance Calder.

And he has Wendy.

Forty-One

I'm shaking.

The smell of cinnamon overpowers my senses.

It's everywhere. In my hair, my clothes, the seats of my car.

I plug "105 Archer Road, Larkhill" into the GPS. It's 23 minutes away.

What does he want from me?

When I get there, will he let her go?

Is he going to kill both of us?

Why is this happening?

He said if I texted anyone, he'd kill her.

I put my phone on the seat beside me and my head on the steering wheel, arms folded in my lap.

How did we get here? Everything has been so good lately.

This is the reason I can't just be happy.

I'm scared.

And this time, I'm angry.

I don't understand his end goal. Revenge feels like the wrong answer.

Vance was one of the board members who pushed the hardest to get the clinical trial through because it was important to him. He never gave off vibes like he was violent.

There were others who, when you looked into their eyes, you could see they were devoid of a soul. That money was their only reason for being in this business.

I never got that feeling from Vance. He always seemed interested in making people's lives better.

I sob while following the GPS's directions.

Wendy has done so much for me, helped me out of the darkest of places, and yet again, I've managed to put her life in danger.

When I get out of the car in Larkhill, I look at the enormous warehouse that I've been guided to in the middle of nowhere.

There isn't a house or building around for miles.

The cinnamon smell is just as strong outside the car.

I put my phone in my purse and bring it with me.

I walk through the door on the side of the building, shaking like never before. I've been scared, but never like this.

This is real terror.

I have no idea what I'm walking into. All around is the evidence of a building that has fallen into disrepair. Rusty desks and chairs are strewn, abandoned, around this large room. The windows are so dirty that you can see the grime even at night. The floors are stained with oil that has sunken deep into the concrete. It's cold, as if the heat is barely working.

I shudder.

Is Wendy hurt?

She must be so scared.

Wendy and Vance aren't in this room. I take a breath and keep walking until I come to another door. I open it and walk through.

"Hi, Della. How've you been?" Vance has a grim look on his face, and I gasp when I see him.

Wendy is handcuffed to a chair, crying. She looks at me, pleading to get her out of this, but doesn't speak.

Is this possible?

How did I not realize?

I start to hyperventilate, and I sit down hard in a rusty chair nearby. He's been here for months, if not longer. It's almost unbelievable.

"I know, Della. I was surprised when you didn't recognize me, too. Have I changed that much?" Now he gives me a sad grin.

He was a good-looking guy years ago, back when he served on the board at ChemGen. Today, he's skinny, shaved bald, and wearing a goatee. He looks exhausted, like life has worn him thin.

"I got the surprise of my life when I came home that night, and you were in the foyer at my building. Well, my short-term residence, anyway." He looks at me and smiles, but there's no joy in it.

I close my eyes hard. I can't believe I didn't see it. That night, he was balding but had some hair and no facial hair. I still should have recognized him. I should have seen what was coming.

It was right in front of me, and I missed it.

Or did I ignore it?

He gets up and takes my purse, rummaging through it. He pulls out my phone, double-checking that I haven't made any calls or sent any texts. When he's sure I didn't, he smashes it on the floor.

"I was so sure that my plans had been ruined that night, that you had found me, recognized me. I had taken so many precautions, tracked you for months while I was setting up. I thought it was over. But the Marshals didn't come."

He looks back into my purse and takes out my wallet. He waves it around as he talks.

"When they didn't show, I was surprised. I couldn't believe that in your rush to get out of there, you barely looked at me. So, I fully shaved my head." He looks at me grimly.

"I needed to track your movements and didn't want to risk you recognizing me from that night. If you had, you'd put the pieces together, and this would be over for me. I've been growing the goatee; do you like it?" He smiles again, still looking very sad. "I visited you at Sanderson's a few times to confirm you didn't recognize me. You didn't."

He pulls my license out of my purse. "Leah Mercer. Hmmm. Could they have given you a plainer name? It doesn't suit you, Della." Just then, he spots something else in my purse. A tin of peppermints. He takes them out and pops one into his mouth.

I remember he always liked those.

I'm still silent. I can't find the words to ask why I'm here, why he's kidnapped Wendy.

"That Carla woman didn't help this process along, either. I was forced to pull back when she started to escalate. She was a real thorn in my side; delayed me for no good reason."

He looks at me and sighs, long and slow. "I almost had you once before, Della. This could have been over months ago. You were walking your dog in the woods by the lake. I had tracked you, and I nearly had you. I was so close, I just needed you a little closer to the road. Then that goddamn friend of yours showed up! It was the last chance I had before the rest of your life went haywire, and you became completely unpredictable." He pops two more mints into his mouth.

That day in the woods. It wasn't Mina's camera lens. It was him.

I'm completely stunned. I knew something was wrong, and I ignored it so I could convince myself I was safe.

Wendy is in trouble so I could feel all warm and fuzzy.

"Nothing to say, Della?" He props one leg up on a chair and leans on it, ensuring I have a clear view of the gun holstered at his hip.

Finally, I find some words. "Why are we here? Are you looking for revenge because I testified?" It doesn't make sense even as I say it out loud.

I shake my head. "It doesn't matter, you have me now. Please let Wendy go." I'm shaking and trying not to cry. I'm trying to be brave and do the right thing for the first time in my life.

He gives a short laugh, but there's no humor in it. "No, Della, I'm not here for revenge."

I look at him, stumped. "I don't understand. If you aren't here to hurt me, us, why are you here?" I feel like he's telling the truth.

"I'm here for the serum." He looks at me very seriously, like everything depends on what I say next.

"What? I... I don't understand. What serum?" He can't be looking for NVX-201. The last of it was destroyed years ago after ChemGen lost in court. And why on earth would he think I have it?

He turns the chair and sits on it backwards, facing me. "The serum, Della. I need you to make it." He still looks serious, but there's a faint ray of... what is it... hope? behind his eyes.

I look at him like he's lost it while throwing my hands up. "Vance, how am I supposed to just make NVX-201? It's not like making a batch of cookies. I don't understand what you want from me."

I would need beakers, pipettes, a list of specialized ingredients, a centrifuge... I would need a fully stocked lab. It isn't possible. Not to mention the numerous ethical concerns.

"Do you know what you're asking of me? Not only is it completely unethical, but I'd need an entire lab to make it happen. It isn't possible, even if I wanted to do it."

I can't believe this.

What could he even want with the serum?

He gets up from the chair and walks over to another door, motioning for me to follow him.

He opens it, and I peer inside. It's a full lab. He must have spent weeks setting this up.

"I have all the material, the scope and access to all the files and prior results. I have everything, Della. You're going to make the serum for me. If you don't, both you and your friend are going to die."

He says it calmly, as if he's rehearsed it over and over again. Calm as he sounds, he's starting to sweat. Small beads of moisture hug his hairline and under his nose.

"I don't understand. The serum hurt people, some of them severely. What do you want with it?"

I'm confused, but an idea strikes me. "Novagenix is recreating an updated formula; I read about it. Their clinical trials start in less than six months."

He lets out a long, heavy sigh, as though I've disappointed him.

What am I missing?

Something is off, and I can't read him.

He talks slowly, as if he's explaining to a child. "You're such a smart woman, Della, but it's amazing how blind you can be." He takes his phone out of his pocket and shows me a picture. It's a photo of a boy, about nine years old. Half of his face has the droop of paralysis.

"Oh my God," I say, swaying slightly. I feel woozy. "This is why the board pushed the trial so hard. Why all of you *insisted* that the clinical trial cover ages five and up. All of those kids were guinea pigs to you, while you were looking for the holy grail of a cure for your own son."

I look at him, angry now. "This is why you tried to push the horrible results under the rug, why you wanted to continue even though you knew it could, would, hurt more people."

Now I'm standing up tall, tall as I can, though I'm still afraid. I refuse to let anyone steer my life anymore.

Vance looks shocked, as if he had never considered the other people who were hurt. His sweating has become more obvious. There are minor stains on the underarms and neckline of his T-shirt.

"They were not guinea pigs," he says softly, not meeting my stare. "But I would do anything for my son. To protect him." He looks back and meets my eyes. "I need this serum. And you're going to make it for me. Because even though you don't value your own life, you value hers." He points to Wendy, who looks shrunken, terrified, tethered to the chair.

"Vance, I'm sorry for your son. I truly am. I can't imagine the pain you've been through. But you have other options. The other trial opens in six months. You don't need me, especially now."

I know now that I need to keep him talking.

"Tim is 10, and the trial is only for adults. Thanks to you and your testimony. You're going to do this. Make the serum."

He's now sweating profusely, like he understands that this isn't going to be as easy as it was in his imagination.

The thing that he doesn't understand is that I'm not who I once was.

I'm not the woman that he and the other nine board members bullied into making the biggest mistake of her career three years ago. I've learned a lot of hard lessons.

Nan told me that to find my way forward, I had to find my way home. I have. And nobody is going to take it away from me.

"You're sweating an awful lot, Vance. Are you nervous?" I'm scared out of my wits but manage to maintain my composure.

He's sitting down now, slightly slumped in the chair. "What are you talking about? You're the one who should be nervous." He points to Wendy half-heartedly. "She's going to get hurt. I'm serious." He looks physically ill.

"Vance, you know the drugs we manufactured pretty well. Do you remember CLM-16?" Everything in me says to untie Wendy and run as fast as we can, but I know I have to wait if I want this to be the end of the madness.

"What?" He's confused. "What are you talking about? What does this have to do with the serum?" His eyes have started to glaze over.

"Maybe you know it by its prescription name, Somnexil? It's what we used to sedate the large animals in the lab when we needed to draw blood. It would put a gorilla down in 30 seconds. Do you know what a small dose does to a human?"

Wendy had given me a fair bit of a hard time filling the prescription, especially in liquid form. But thankfully, she trusts me enough to know that even if I'm a mental case, I'm now one that has solid backup plans.

Vance still looks confused, especially because he's probably trying his hardest to stay conscious.

"How did you like my mints?"

I stare at him now. There's no joy for me in drugging him, but I'm beyond relieved that this worked.

Realization hits him no more than an instant before he passes out and slumps to the floor.

I look at him sadly.

I really do feel terrible for him and his son. But I couldn't help him. Not this way.

I'm shaking again, a mix of terror and relief. "Wendy, do you know where the keys to those cuffs are?" I'm searching the table nearby.

"No, but we need to get out of here! I'll drag the chair behind me, and we can worry about the cuffs later. Let's go!"

"It's okay," I tell her. "He'll be out for a solid 30 minutes, and help will be here long before then. I promise, we're safe."

I've gotten very, very good at having backup plans in place.

"Help? What are you talking about? He smashed your phone. I watched him." She's looking at me incredulously, like I've finally lost it.

I calmly reach down and lift my pant leg. In a small holster is a burner phone. "I have six of them stashed everywhere you can think of. The back seat of my car, my room. One sewn into the lining of my purse. One at Sanderson's. Also Root. This is number six," I say, taking it out of its holster. It had been Velcroed under my steering wheel. It has one preprogrammed text that's auto-set up to send to Mina with a single button push.

It happened. Track me. #6

Forty-Two

Within two minutes, Mina and the U.S. Marshals swarm the place. They free Wendy, and we huddle together, half in disbelief that it's actually over.

Vance is still unconscious as they put him in the back of an ambulance. He'll wake up at the hospital and then be transported to jail. He'll go to prison for his previous crimes, but he'll also be facing new charges of kidnapping and attempted murder. He may never see the outside of a cell again.

I hurt for him, even now.

But I was not going to recreate the serum, especially with Wendy's life hanging in the balance.

Mina comes over and hugs us. "I'm so glad you got to one of the phones, Ellie. I was terrified getting the text, but I immediately contacted the Marshals with the information, and we were on our way in under 10 minutes." She looks immensely relieved.

Wendy is still in shock. "I'm so glad I gave you that prescription. I can't believe I argued with you about it. It saved us." She breaks down crying again, wracking sobs that shake her entire body.

I hug her, squeezing her tight. "I'm so sorry that I got you into this, but I promise it's over now. There's no more hiding, no more need for witness protection. I'm safe. *We're* safe."

I hate that I got her involved, but I'm so grateful that it's over now.

Deputy U.S. Marshal Pratt says they'll need us for statements tomorrow, but it's an open-and-shut case, and we can go home.

It's close to midnight as we go outside. The winter air is frigid and stings my nose as I breathe in. I take another deep breath and let it heal me.

Mina drives my car home. I'm in the passenger seat; Wendy's in the back. She glances at me, and I smile, thinking of the first night we "met."

This moment feels like everything is coming full circle.

Forty-Three

By May, Wendy's house is rebuilt, and we "officially" move in together. She's happy to have her new kitchen.

Maisie is happy to have her fenced yard again, and I'm truly thankful for where I am today.

I've changed in ways I could never have imagined, and though I'm still more anxious than most people, I've stopped looking over my shoulder.

She decides to host a "Housewarming—Matches not included" party and invites at least 50 people from town.

Bill and Mina are obviously on the guest list.

I walk around the party, meeting new people. I say hello to others I never took the time to get to know.

I laugh at a joke someone tells, then drift over to a conversation about politics.

When it gets heated, I take my leave and talk with someone about my newly formed business, *Second Light Homeopathics*. It's going well, and I love everything about what I do now.

I work part-time at Sanderson's, usually two shifts a week, sometimes more.

Bill's business is still booming.

Spotting him across the room, I walk over to check on him.

"Hey, Bill, how's it going?"

He shows me the online gallery he's put together of his artwork. It's incredible that he actually has fans. He's found the perfect niche community for his hobby.

I look at his pictures, and we laugh about the things that have brought him to this point.

I spot Mina across the room and tell Bill we'll finish catching up later.

I sidle up to her and poke her with my elbow. "Having fun?" She's relaxed a lot, at least with Wendy and me.

"It's a nice party," she says, dodging the question and gripping her glass of champagne.

Wendy and I are her best friends, and she still struggles with trusting new people. It's something that we have in common.

I sip my glass of champagne, feeling relaxed.

I know that if something were to happen, I'm prepared now.

The party continues into the evening without issues. At the end of the night, it's just me, Wendy and Mina sitting on the couch in the living room, finishing the last of the champagne.

Wendy pulls a blanket over herself. "Man, I'm tired! What a long day. It was fun, though!" She is ever the people person, the optimist. Even with everything she's been through, she still loves and trusts people in a way I'll never really understand. It's one of the best things about her.

"Well, I'm headed to bed. You guys staying up a bit?" She yawns and gets up from the couch.

"Yeah, I'm going to stay up a bit," I tell her. I turn to Mina. "You going to stay a while?"

"Sure, I've got nothing else going on." She's always ready to hang out. I think if Wendy had another bedroom, she probably would have moved in, too.

Wendy says goodnight and shuffles off to bed, still yawning.

There's something that's been on my mind for a while, and I haven't said it out loud to anyone. "Mina, can I tell you something? Will you tell me if I sound crazy?" I look at her tentatively.

She laughs. "You can tell me anything, and yes, you know I'll tell you if you sound crazy. It wouldn't be the first time."

I reach into my pocket, pulling out a pair of safety scissors.

Mina looks at me, confused. "Where did you get those?"

I turn them over in my hands. "Found them near the shelf a couple of days before it fell on me. I know, right now I sound like I've lost it, but stick with me."

She smiles at me and rolls her eyes.

Next, I pull out my phone. "I've watched this video more times than I can count. Maybe I'm imagining things." I press play.

If you back the camera footage up two minutes from the night of the fire, there's what looks like a small shadow that passes on the left side. It looks like someone very short is sneaking up to the house, just out of view. Fast-forward, and you see Carla running up the driveway, passing right under the camera.

The look on her face isn't anger or determination: it's fear.

Fast-forward again, and you see Carla through the smoke, walking away. If you pause, you can almost make out the outline of a second body—a small one.

Mina watches, then rewinds and watches again. "It can't be." She looks disturbed.

I understand; I feel the same way.

"That's why I'm asking. I honestly don't know if I'm crazy."

I pull a small piece of wire from my other pocket. "I had someone look at this, too. It's a piece of a violin string."

Mina looks at me, shocked. "What? It... it's not possible. It just can't be. Can it?"
Can it?

Epilogue

I'm standing on the platform, waiting. It's a beautiful, sunny summer day. There's a gentle breeze that blows a piece of blonde hair across my face.

The breeze dries the light sheen of sweat on my shoulders as the sun filters through the cracks in the wooden overhang. Everything smells of lilac and early summer heat, lending an ethereal feel to the day.

I breathe out a sigh of absolute serenity. Life could not be sweeter right now.

It's been about 18 months since the fire, and everyone I know is now in a good place, both emotionally and physically.

Mina is standing next to me, looking nervous.

I squeeze her hand.

She doesn't need to be; it's going to be great.

She left her job to start her own crisis management company, which is mostly remote work.

She travels a few times a year for on-site training, but she makes plenty of money, and the flexibility is fantastic.

Her dad passed late last year, and it was really rough for her, but she's healing slowly.

Her mom is now in assisted living and, honestly, doing great.

She moved in with Wendy and me about six months ago, and it's great to have her so close.

Honestly, she practically lived there anyway. It only made sense.

Wendy would be here, but Root is thriving these days.

Bill taught her some of his tricks, and though her marketing strategies are less, well... gimmicky, they've taken off.

Her online sales have skyrocketed. She has my products to thank for some of it, but most of it was her own doing.

Maisie goes to work with her a couple of days a week. She's the store mascot now, and everyone in town loves her. She loves the extra pets and treats she gets for being a good girl.

Bill eventually met his online friend, Maggie. She's perfect for him in every way. She loves trying new things, so she gets Bill out of the house almost every weekend. They play pool on Friday nights, they've gone parasailing, and they even hosted a "paint night" at the store.

He's happier than I've ever seen him.

I've healed in ways I never thought possible. I still have my coping mechanisms, but they feel more like habit now than anxiety.

I started seeing a therapist a few months ago, and she's helping me unpack my many layers of trauma.

I don't feel quite as burdened with it all as I used to.

We hear the train whistle, then watch it slowly pull into the station.

As it slows to a stop, the faint smell of diesel fuel and warm metal floats across the platform.

The doors open and people rush out. The platform is suddenly busy and filled with the hustle and bustle of people rushing to their next destination.

As the rush slows to a more leisurely crawl, we see her emerge from the train car—an older woman with long gray hair, front strands braided and clasped behind her head with a jeweled flower clip—moving gracefully onto the platform.

I run to her, embracing her like I may never get the chance again. Her skin is soft, and she smells of clove and nutmeg.

It's a moment I've dreamed of for nearly two years.

I pull back out of the embrace and hold her at arm's length to look at her for an extra moment.

"Nan," I say, my eyes filling with tears. "Welcome. It is so good to have you here. I've missed you so much."

My old life and new life are finally beginning to merge.

She smiles. "Thank you, Ellie. Thanks for having me." She hugs me again. "I'm so glad you finally found your way home."

She then turns to Mina. "It's so nice to meet you, my dear. I've heard so much about you."

She pulls her in for a hug, too. Mina is taken by surprise but melts into Nan's hug. It's impossible not to.

I pick up Nan's bag, and Mina takes her suitcase.

We walk down from the platform to the parking lot, the breeze whispering and shifting the scent of lilac around us.

I see Mina instinctively scanning the perimeter. She's always on the lookout, ever the protector.

There's no danger here.

At least... not today.

Acknowledgements

Writing a book was, for decades, a pipe dream of mine. One day in 2025. I wrote the first chapter of *I Haven't Been Myself,* then sent it to Tara, Jenny and Kara and asked, word for word, "Am I crazy, or should I keep writing?" Guys, without your enthusiasm, this would never have happened. Thank you.

Without Marc, I would not have had the capacity to keep allowing the words to pour out of me. Thank you for the hours and hours spent entertaining the kids and helping me find pockets of quiet (and sometimes not-so. quiet.) A second thank you for being my acting editor and picking apart the pieces that needed it, even if I wasn't a great sport about it at first.

Thank you to Jami and Janine for being my tried-and-true beta readers and supportive friends. I appreciate your honest feedback and know I'll always get it from the two of you.

Ryder, Mav and Raven, I hope that someday you'll read my books as adults, and it will give you a new perspective on the woman who raised you.

I'd like to thank Gary, my copyeditor, for polishing the book to this level. I tried my best to do it on my own, but you are the one who made it truly professional.

Also, a huge shoutout to Clint for the incredible cover art. Somehow, you managed to catch Leah's very essence without ever turning a single page. You truly have a gift.

Lastly, if you made it this far, thank you so much for reading my first novel. It's a strangely public but very personal thing to put out into the world for complete strangers to read (and hopefully enjoy).

About the Author

Nicole Palermo is a New England-based writer of psychological fiction exploring memory and identity. *I Haven't Been Myself* is her debut novel.

More at NicolePalermoAuthor.com

Coming Soon from Nicole Palermo

What Remains of Her

There's something Nadia is supposed to remember.

Inside a deteriorating institution, her past is rationed in
fragments. The staff call it treatment. She calls it erasure.

When the memories return, they don't bring relief.
They bring consequences.

Coming July 2026.

Sneak Peek of

What Remains of Her

One

There's something I'm supposed to remember.

I'm sure I knew it once. It's long gone now.

I look out the dirty, grime-streaked window. The sky is gray, and you can feel the moisture outside as though you're part of the mist.

Even inside, the world around me is dense and foggy.

I know there are others, but their lines are blurred and distant regardless of proximity.

I look down at my lunch. The tray is still full.

Didn't I eat? I thought I had.

I pick up a slimy peach, and it slides off the fork and back onto the tray.

I don't think I'm very hungry.

"Nadia, you need to eat your lunch," says one of the nurses, looking at my untouched tray. She looks grim, her mouth a straight line. It's like a child drew it in pencil and forgot her lips. Her skin is almost gray. It clashes against the bright white of her uniform.

"I'm not very hungry," I tell her, looking back out the window. It feels brighter out there, despite the gloom.

She sighs heavily. "You know you need to eat some of it. Your meds may suppress your appetite, but we can't have you starve to death." She puts her clipboard down on the table next to me and picks up my fork. She stabs a very overcooked slab of what might be meat and shoves it into my mouth.

I chew obediently. It's not a good idea to argue. Bad things happen when you don't do what you're told. Resisting any part of your treatment plan is grounds for the seclusion room. I don't want to go back there.

She stabs another piece with the fork and tells me to eat it.

When I do, she grabs her clipboard and moves on to the next patient.

I eat a little more on my own. Enough that she won't come back.

There's a distinct smell to the dining hall, like junior high cafeteria meets nursing home. Sweat, body odor, cigarette smoke and cheap meat permeate the area. It's not a pleasant place to be, but if I'm being honest, there isn't a pleasant room in this facility.

The nurse stops by my table again, glancing at my tray to ensure I made an attempt to eat. She nods, seemingly satisfied, and makes a note in my chart before moving on.

I long ago lost track of what day it is, but after lunch, we meet with the doctors in our rooms during rounds.

At least, I think that's what happens after lunch.

I don't correctly remember a lot of the time anymore. Much of my life prior to Ravensbrook Institute has been lost, really.

Occasionally, there are flashes of people or a brief memory that appears, but then my meds kick in, and they're lost again.

I typically spend my days, well, dazed, for lack of a better term. I do my best to play nice and not anger anyone. I've learned it's not a good idea to argue.

I glance around, looking for the others with blurry outlines. Someone I know is sitting two tables over. Betty, I think her name is. Or is it Paula? She sees me looking and gets up, then shuffles over to my table.

"Hey," she says, sliding into the chair across from me. "Did you know this used to be a tuberculosis clinic when it was built? One of those 'wellness retreats' for rich people." She moves her head to look directly into my eyes, to see if I'm paying attention. She's high-strung, and she taps her nails on the table.

"Oh?" I try to sound attentive, but I don't care.

"Yeah, Ravensbrook was built in the 1890s or something. Know how many people it's supposed to hold?" She looks like the cat who ate the canary, like she's holding back a secret she thinks I just can't wait to hear.

"How many?" I wish she'd go away. My head is starting to hurt.

"Just a hundred," she says, frowning. "There's almost four hundred now. I overheard two of the nurses talking." She picks at a cuticle.

"Oh. Wow." I want to go back to my room. The lights here are too bright, and Betty/Paula's voice is making my headache worse.

"Can you believe that? In 80 years, it went from a place for rich people to a loony bin where they drug us to keep us in line. One of these days I'm going to get out of here, I really am." She's agitated now.

I think the nurses may need to up her dosage.

She's quiet for a moment, then blurts out, "Do you hear the screams at night?" She looks at me, wide-eyed.

I think this is what she really wanted to ask me. The information about the building was a segue. "Sometimes," I say truthfully. Occasionally, my meds start to wear off late into the night, and I lie in bed, awake.

I hear the screams, even though I try not to.

Before Betty/Paula can ask another question, a nurse taps my tray and tells me it's time to go back to my room. I stand up slowly. "Bye… Betty," I guess. She doesn't correct me, so either I got it right or she doesn't care.

The world spins for a moment when I stand. Just as it's starting to settle, I feel another tap, this time on my shoulder.

"Get going, Moren, we don't have all day." I think Moren is my last name; they sometimes use it instead of Nadia.

I'll forget it again by tomorrow.

www.ingramcontent.com/pod-product-compliance
Lightning Source LLC
Chambersburg PA
CBHW051310130726
47987CB00004B/1739